ANTONIO MACHADO

Lands of Castile
Campos de Castilla
and other poems

1. Pen and ink drawing depicting Antonio Machado
with the Alcázar of Segovia in the background.
(José Tablada Martín, 1994)

ANTONIO MACHADO

Lands of Castile
Campos de Castilla
and other poems

Translated with introduction and notes by

Paul Burns & Salvador Ortiz-Carboneres

My childhood is memories of a courtyard in Seville
And a sunlit garden with ripening lemons;
my youth, twenty years in the lands of Castile;
my story, some events I would rather not tell.
Portrait (poem XCVII, p.47)

Aris & Phillips Hispanic Classics

are published by

Oxbow Books, Park End Place, Oxford OX1 1HN

First published in Great Britain by Aris & Phillips Ltd, 2002.

Reprinted with corrections 2006.

ISBN 0-85668-743-X

A CIP record for this book is available from the British Library.

Printed and bound by CPI Group (UK) Ltd, Croydon, CR0 4YY

Contents

List of Illustrations

Misterioso y silencioso
iba una y otra vez.
Su mirada era tan profunda
que apenas se podía ver.
Cuando hablaba tenía un dejo
de timidez y altivez
y la luz de sus pensamientos
casi siempre se veía arder.

Mysterious and silent,
he came and he went.
His gaze was so deep
it could hardly be seen.
His speech had a touch
of shyness and pride
and the light of his thoughts
nearly always glowed bright.

Rubén Darío

Preface

The "immediate" inspiration for this book was the publication by Burns & Oates in 1993 of a Spanish/English text of the *Poems of St John of the Cross*, translated by Kathleen Jones. Salvador saw this and wrote to me proposing that he and I work together on a selection of poems by Antonio Machado, to be published in the same format. My reply was that Machado, though a personal favourite, was not really a religious poet first and foremost (despite the themes of absence and presence of God in his work) and therefore not suitable for the predominantly Catholic imprint of Burns & Oates. I also said I was just embarking on what looked like a five-year stint on Lives of the Saints and would he please come back after that. He did.

For both of us, love of Machado goes a long way farther back. For me, it started during my first visit to Madrid, in 1950, when Machado was politically hardly a name to be produced in the open. The family with whom I had the good fortune to stay, however, were deeply cultured, enthusiasts for the *romance* tradition, as Machado himself was, and not such as allow themselves to be fettered in their appreciation by political constraints. They also lived a hundred yards from one of Machado's favourite Madrid haunts, the Café Gijón. My much-travelled and annotated first copy of what were then published —in Buenos Aires— as the *Poesías Completas* dates from my first term at Oxford in 1954. I returned to Madrid for a year between the second and third years of my Oxford course —a guinea pig in those days, though the year abroad is considered essential now. From Madrid I explored much of the lands of Castile on a Vespa, but it was not until 1988 that I first went to Soria. By then Machado had been rehabilitated and become a tourist attraction: a *parador* had been built on the site of the old castle and named after him; sites associated with his poems had copies of them on walls or trees. We lunched at Cidones Inn (see Poem CXVII, p. 67) and climbed up to the Black Lagoon at the source of the Duero in the majestic Sierra de Urbión. I was inspired to write an article on "a prophet with honour in his country," with translations of some poems, but failed to find an outlet for it. Salvador's suggestion five years later fell, therefore, on partially tilled soil.

I had not kept pace with English translations that had appeared over the decades but Salvador had and was convinced there was still a good case for a new attempt. Generally, he (the native Spanish speaker) supplied a first draft, I (the native English speaker) did what I could to achieve a tolerable rhythm, and versions went back and forth until we were both happy. We have not attempted to impose rhyme: the assonance of Spanish endings simply will not pass into English. Machado's strength is in his simplicity (which conceals a consummate art and knowledge of Spanish metrical forms); we have aimed to reproduce this above all. As he himself said, he eschews anecdote: he observes and records, and this applies to life and landscape. He asserts rather than describes, with a pinpoint accuracy in his use of nouns and adjectives. We had to go to Castile to test our words against the reality, and we met for the first time in April 2001, to spend a few very productive days in Soria and Segovia.

From this visit, our thanks are due to the Instituto Histórico Provincial in Soria for the period photographs that appear here. The Casa-Museo Antonio Machado in Segovia shows the stark simplicity of Machado's life, especially in his preserved bedroom, and the guide and bookseller, César Gutiérrez Gómez, could not have been more supportive. My cousin Tom Burns Marañón and his wife Dolores provided not only hospitality but also the —almost miraculous— information that Machado's great-niece (her mother being his youngest brother Francisco's daughter) lived a few doors away: Doña Mercedes Lecea Machado was gracious enough to see me at short notice and provide some illuminating family memories, which I have used to add a couple of personal touches to the outline of his life in the Introduction.

We should also, on behalf of the publishers, like to express thanks to Don José Rollán Riesco, executive for the heirs of Antonio Machado, who took some tracking down but then agreed sensible (indeed generous) terms for the use of the Spanish text and permission to translate. The Spanish text used is that of the latest edition of the *Poesías Completas*, edited by Manuel Alvar and published by Espasa Calpe of Madrid in their Colección Austral in 2000. With a long and excellent introduction, extra poems discovered over the years, added documentation, and a "reading workshop" the volume has grown to over 500 pages and is three times as thick as my 1954 Losada edition. Quite early on in this collaboration, we submitted a selection to Dr Jean Boise-Beier at the School of Language, Linguistics and Translation Studies at the University of East Anglia for inclusion in the British Comparative Literature Association/British Centre for Literary Translation competition for the year 2000. We were quite pleased to receive a commendation with the note that "the overall standard of entries was extremely high, and the judges were impressed with your work." A further encouragement was the acceptance of two poems, *Portrait* (Poem XCVII, pp. 45-46) and *On the Banks of the Duero* (Poem XCVIII, pp. 47-51) for publication in *Modern Poetry in Translation*. and these appeared in its No. 18, New Series, *European Voices* (Sept. 2001), pp. 83-6.

Last and very definitely not least, our thanks go to our publishers for their decision to accept this venture as an addition to their "Hispanic Classics" series and for their enthusiasm, suggestions, various skills, and hospitality. As a publisher myself, I know how publishers should treat authors, and they measure up very well.

Paul Burns   *Stowell, July 2001*

Introduction

Background

Antonio Machado lived during some of Spain's most turbulent decades, and these left echoes in his poetry. He was part of a generation that was inextricably bound up with the fate of the country, and he was to become its most characteristic poet. As the history of Spain played such an influential role in his life, and as Spain's modern history has been in many respects so different from that of the rest of Europe, it seems sensible (if unfashionable in a postmodernist world) to start by placing him in his historical context.

Spain in the Nineteenth Century

At the beginning of the nineteenth century the Napoleonic Wars and the destruction of the Spanish fleet at Trafalgar, near Gibraltar, had left Spain's national fortunes at an extremely low ebb. In 1808 King Charles IV was forced by a union of aristocrats and officers to abdicate in favour of his son Ferdinand. The new king was escorted through cheering crowds to the royal palace in Madrid by French troops under General Murat, but it soon became apparent that the French intent was to do away with the Bourbon monarchy altogether and settle the Bonapartes on the throne. Ferdinand abdicated, while the populace turned from a mood of collaboration with the French to one of resistance, which was savagely put down, as Goya's *Executions of 3 May 1808* bears witness for all time.

The executions in Madrid provoked uprisings all over Spain, producing what are known as the Spanish Wars of Independence. Without a king or a central government, Spanish irregular forces (which gave rise to the term *guerrilla*) had inflicted defeats on the French in Catalonia and at the great battle of Bailén in July, proving that Napoleon's forces were no longer invincible. Napoleon then embarked on a full-scale invasion of Spain, causing the British to intervene in what they called the Peninsular War, with its heroic disaster of the retreat of Sir John Moore to Corunna and his burial there —"Not a drum was heard, not a funeral note . . ."— followed by Wellington's more successful and brutal campaign. Spanish forces put up heroic resistance against the French in cities such as Gerona and Zaragoza, the spirit of the latter caught in a popular ballad:

La Vírgen del Pilar dice *que no quiere ser francesa;* *que prefiere ser capitana* *de la tropa aragonesa.*	Says the Virgin of the Pillar: To France I'll not belong; I'd rather be a captain of the troops of Aragon.

Wellington liberated Madrid in August 1812, and in that year the Cortes met in Cadiz to promulgate a new and more democratic Constitution for the country —the first of many swings toward a more liberal and secular Spain that, with their corresponding repressions, were to culminate in the Spanish Civil War of 1936-9: Machado's "man in a provincial casino" in *The Ephemeral Past* (Poem CXXXI, pp. 77-79) "forecasts that the liberals will come/as storks return to their bell tower." The traditional powers in Spain were beginning to lose their grip on their nation and colonies. The spirit of independence spread to Spain's South American empire, where "liberators" such as Bolívar and San Martín redrew the colonial map and effectively founded the nation states that remain to this day.

The Bourbons returned to the throne, once again in the unattractive person of Ferdinand VII —"a blot on our history," as José de Espronceda called him. He refused to ratify the new Constitution, dissolved parliament, and reinstated the Inquisition. Ferdinand's abuses of the common people led to another national uprising: troops garrisoned in Andalusia preparing to embark to quell independence movements in South America rose up at Las Cabezas de San Juan. They were eventually defeated by the arrival of the royalist French force known as the Hundred Thousand Sons of St Louis.

Ferdinand died in 1833, having abolished the Salic Law so that his daughter Isabella, still a child, could inherit the throne. His disinherited brother Carlos raised arms in the separatist northern regions —the Basque Country, Navarre, Aragon, and Catalonia— and thereby initiated the First Carlist War. This lasted seven years, ending with the treaty of Vergara (1839) between the Carlists, whose stance was reactionary absolutist, and the Regent, María Cristina, who might be seen as the lesser of two evils. In August 1836 María Cristina and her lover, Muñoz, were trying to escape the war in the palace of La Granja when members of her personal guard presented her with a liberal Constitution. It took a threat to her lover's life to induce her to sign the document. The Constitution, promulgated in 1837, attempted to reconcile personal freedoms with monarchical privilege.

Under María Cristina's succesor, Isabella II (1833-64), who was declared of age in 1843, Spain went through a period of unrest, with Isabella's authoritarian rule upheld by Generals Narváez and the slightly more moderate O'Donnell. The unrest was increasingly directed at Isabella personally, whose scandalous personal life did not help her cause any more than did her arbitrary attempts to interfere in government. After the deaths of Narváez in 1867 and O'Donnell in 1868, her position became untenable, and a revolution in the autumn of 1868 threw her off the throne. A provisional government, attempting to reconcile individual liberty with Spanish traditional values, aimed to restore the monarchy but had difficulty in choosing who should be king. It proclaimed Amadeus of Savoy king in 1870, but he abdicated after only two years. The First Republic was proclaimed on 11 February 1873, but this lasted a mere eleven months, during which it had four presidents.

A *coup d'état* by General Pavía restored the monarchy in the person of Alfonso, who reigned as Alfonso XII from 1874 (the year before Antonio Machado was born) to 1885. His mother returned from exile in Paris to interfere, but she was generally thwarted and under Alfonso and with some wise first ministers, both conservative and liberal, the country enjoyed a spell of relative calm. After the king's death, his widow, another María Cristina, acted as regent until 1902.

Loss of Colonies and the Generation of '98

In 1898 Spain went to war with the United States in an attempt to cling to its last remaining New World colonies: Cuba, Puerto Rico, and the Philippines. The fading European colonial power was never going to be any match for the emergent hegemonic power in the New World, and despite the heroism shown by Spanish naval detachments off Havana and Manila, defeat was inevitable. The resulting despair was followed by an intellectual renaissance, led by a group of writers known as the Generation of '98. "Two Spains" —one traditionalist, imperialistic, centralist, and Catholic; the other humanist, liberal, federal, and anticlerical— had been tearing the country apart for centuries: according to some commentators, since before the Roman occupation or at least since the first Gothic king, Ataulf, in the fifth century; according to others, since the sixteenth or eighteenth centuries.

In his *Idearium español* (1897) the essayist Angel Ganivet tries to identify permanent features of Spain and laments that the country "never manages to transform itself, to find a more peaceful, ideal means of expression and to speak in more human ways than with arms."[1] The philosopher, poet, and novelist Miguel de Unamuno saw the "comically tragic figure" of Don Quixote embodying the "immortal soul of my people" and saw the heartland of Castile as its inspiration. José Ortega y Gasset took the opposite view and urged Spain to look to modern Europe, since "the old Spain, with its governing and governed classes, is now dying." He was later (1930) to spell this out in what might have

---

1   Angel Ganivet, *Idearium español*, in *Obras Completas* (Madrid: Aguilar, 1961). Trans. Jimmy Burns in *Spain: A Literary Guide* (London: John Murray, 1994), p. 152.

been an early blueprint for a federalist project of the European Union: "Only the determination to construct a great nation from the group of peoples of the Continent would give a new life to the pulse of Europe."[2] José Martínez Ruiz, writing under the pen name "Azorín" (see Poem CXVII, p. 64) saw the two Spains as a "perpetual tumult of opposing passions," with the masses clamouring for liberty on the one hand and the *caudillo* figure imposing control on the other.[3] (This is, however, somewhat simplistic, as the industrial working class was numerically and geographically very limited, and the peasant population had tended to support the *status quo*.)

While the philosophers and writers debated and wrote, the army became progressively involved in an unwinnable war in Morocco, which led to the annihilation of a Spanish army in the Rif Valley in 1921. Urban workers periodically organized strikes and took to the barricades in the name of anarchy, socialism, or communism, most notably in Barcelona in 1912. In 1923 General Primo de Rivera, with the support of the army, imposed a military dictatorship, which managed to secure peace in Morocco and undertook a wide programme of public works. Its "one party" view of the State was, however, hardly the unifying force the country needed. Alfonso XIII, who reigned from 1902 to 1930 (though in name only with Primo de Rivera in power), similarly failed to unite the country. Received by Pope Pius XI in 1923, he assured the Pope that "Spain maintained the Spain of Philip II, which battled in the name of the Church" and quoted his consecration of the country to the Sacred Heart of Jesus as evidence that the whole country was behind him in this vision. The Pope did not thank him for this view, expressing instead the wish that "the Spain which did not conform to those views should be borne in mind."[4] Needless to say, it was not.

Republic, Revolution, Civil War

¿Y qué vendrá después? Tal la pregunta	And what will come next? That's the question
que se hacen en España los borregos	the yearlings of the coward flock are asking
del rebaño cobarde y luego ciegos	themselves in Spain, then blindly walking
marchan a paso de cansada yunta	at the pace of a tired yoke of oxen.

This prophetic question, with its savage answer, was asked by Miguel de Unamuno, writing from exile under the dictatorship. Primo de Rivera fell from power in 1930 and Alfonso XIII left the country in 1931, ushering in yet another swing

---

2   José Ortega y Gasset, *La rebelión de las masas* (Madrid, 1930; new ed. Espasa Calpe, 1976), trans. in Burns, p. 153.
3   "Azorín," cited in Burns, p. 150.
4   Ramón Menéndez Pidal, *The Spaniards in Their History*, trans. Walter Starkie (New York: W. W. Norton, 1950), p. 243.

towards a liberal, more European Spain. This too failed to unite the country, as it employed a triumphalist populist and anti-Catholic discourse as divisive as that of the king and the strong leader. Manuel Azaña, the first prime minister of the Republican government, "proclaimed that Catholic Spain had ceased to exist on the exact day, the twelfth of April 1931, when the Republicans triumphed in the elections."[5] The next five years were a more rapid and violent replay of the earlier swings from left to right. The origins of the war are complex and disputed, and have been much written about.[6] Elections in 1933 produced a right-wing alliance, overturned by a radical left-wing coalition early in 1936, with popular local uprisings all over the country. Right-wing politicians conspired with elements representing the bulk of the armed forces, and General Franco led a military uprising (or "national crusade," as he preferred to call it) in July 1936. The left-wing elements responded by putting their areas under the control of Workers' Committees, which proceeded to round up and execute priests, monks and nuns and anyone suspected of "bourgeois" sympathies —meaning even the moderately wealthy and those seen as connected with the Church. Where they took control, the Nationalists embarked on an "anti-Red" campaign of at least equal savagery. The Soviet Union supported the Republic but undermined its government by creating a parallel communist structure of command; Fascist Italy and Nazi Germany used Spain as a testing ground for their new weaponry and as a preparation for the Second World War. Picasso's portrayal of the devastating effect of aerial bombing of civil targets, in his mural *Guernica*, provided an icon of the Civil War comparable in power to that produced by Goya of the Wars of Independence.

One of the "Two Spains" triumphed in 1939 and denied existence to the other (though on a diminishing scale of violence) until Franco died in 1975. Since then, Spain's general tendency has been in the direction of Ortega's European vision, though not without strong separatist tensions. Standards of living have risen to the general western European level; the Catholic Church has lobbied successfully for the canonization of hundreds of "martyrs" in the Civil War. At the same time this Church has contributed hugely to the current of thought known as liberation theology, still suspected of Marxism by the Vatican. There finally appears to be a reasonable prospect of Ramón Menéndez Pidal's view being widely endorsed by the Spanish people and their leaders: "To suppress those who think differently and crush projects for what our brothers believe to

5   Ibid.
6   The most comprehensive account in English is Hugh Thomas, *The Spanish Civil War* (London: Hamish Hamilton, 1977). Classic eyewitness and other works include George Orwell's *Homage to Catalonia* (London: Secker & Warburg, 1938), Gerald Brenan's *The Spanish Labyrinth* (London: Cambridge University Press, 1964), and Arthur Koestler's *Spanish Testament* (London: Gollancz, 1937).

be a better life, is to sin against prudence."[7] Antonio Machado, who lost his life as one such project was crushed, would have agreed wholeheartedly with this view.

Machado's Life

Parents; Seville; Memories

Antonio Machado Ruiz was born in Seville on 29 July 1875. On the subject of his early years in Seville he simply states: "I was born one July night in 1875, in the famous Palacio de las Dueñas, situated in the street of the same name. My memories of the city I was born in are all those of a child, since at the age of eight I went to Madrid, to where my parents moved. . . ." (*Prologue*, 1917). This received its poetic expression in the opening couplet of his *Portrait* (Poem CXVII, p. 45):

My childhood is memories of a courtyard in Seville
and a sunlit garden with ripening lemons.

The Palacio de las Dueñas belonged to the Dukes of Alba, but by the late nineteenth century it had been divided into separate apartments, one of which the Machado family occupied. His father, a lawyer, looked after the current duke's interests.

Machado was never exactly expansive on the subject of his life: "My story, some events I would rather not tell" (*ibid.*). Through one of his "masks" he does, nevertheless, take us back to the occasion of his parents' first meeting: "It happened that some dolphins, mistaking their course and carried by the tide, had come up the Guadalquivir as far as Seville. From all over the city people flocked to the river banks to see this unfamiliar sight; little ladies and swells, among them those who were my parents, who saw each other there for the first time."[8] Antonio Machado Alvarez and Ana Ruiz were married on 22 May 1873, and they named their eldest child Manuel. He was also to be a distinguished poet, defined by Antonio as representing "modernism" and "lyric impressionism"; the third, José, became a painter of note. Antonio, the second son, attended the elementary school run by one Antonio Sánchez.

Madrid, Paris

In 1883 Antonio's grandfather was appointed to a chair at the Central University, and the family moved to Madrid. There Antonio and Manuel went

7   Ramón Menéndez Pidal, *The Spaniards in the Their History*, p. 244.
8   Antonio Machado, *Juan de Mairena (Para la biografía de Mairena)*, vol. 2 (Buenos Aires: Losada, 1957), cited in J. G. Manrique de Lara, *Antonio Machado* (Barcelona, Bilbao, Madrid, Valencia: Unión Editorial, 1968).

to the *Instituto Libre de Enseñanza*, the "free teaching institute," an independent school founded in 1876 by Francisco Giner de los Ríos (see Poem CXXXIX, p. 85)

This rapidly became the intellectual focus of liberal, humanist Spain (and, in the climate of the country, therefore inevitably anticlerical if not outright anti-Catholic). Machado comments: "I still have a lively affection for and deep gratitude to its teachers" (*Prologue*, 1917). Again, he says little about his younger days: "My youth, twenty years in the lands of Castile" (*Portrait*); "My adolescence and youth belong to Madrid" (*Prologue*).

Antonio continued to live at home after the deaths of his father and grandfather in the 1890s. His father died in 1893 after taking up a post in Puerto Rico as property registràr for the Duke of Alba, which was supposed to improve the fragile family fortunes. He had been ill for some years and was forced to return to Seville, where he died without seeing his children again. Antonio took up his further education, after a long break, at the *Instituto de San Isidro* and then the *Instituto Cardenal Cisneros*. He read Bécquer's *Leyendas*, and the novels of Dickens and the plays of Shakespeare in translation. He undertook freelance writing and editorial assignments, including work on a French-Spanish dictionary, which took him to Paris in 1899. There Antonio joined his brother Manuel and worked in the distinguished publishing house of Garnier for several months. He was in France for the brilliant Paris Exhibition of 1900, which left a deep impression on him. He met Oscar Wilde, the Basque novelist Pío Baroja, and other literary notables, but he was apparently not particularly impressed by

2. General view of Soria around the time of Antonio's stay.

the *fin de siècle* intellectual climate of the Paris of the Dreyfuss Affair. By then, Spain had lost its last American colonies in the brief and disastrous 1898 war against the United States, which produced the *Generación del '98*.

On his return from Paris, Antonio spent some months as an actor, and in 1900 he received his Bachelor's degree. His first published poems appeared in 1901 in the review *Electra*, founded the year before. In 1903, his first collection, *Soledades*, was published. He returned to Paris for several months in 1902, and during this stay met the great (and fashionable) Nicaraguan poet Rubén Darío, otherwise known as the founder of Modernism, whom Machado described as "neo-Baroque." Darío was later to be far more forthcoming in his verbal portrait of Machado: "Antonio Machado is perhaps the most intense of all. . . . I knew him long ago, in youthful nights of beer and lyricism. The silent one became talkative and a noble, sparkling conversationalist. Sallies and paradox came easily to him. . . . His look of an unkempt young lord seemed armoured with resignation, and his paradox and sally were always tempered with indulgence."[9] These observations were put even more pithily in the poem that was used as an epigraph to the 1946 edition of Machado's collected poems and from which some lines are similarly used in this selection.

Soria. Leonor

Antonio had little family money behind him, and writing was a precarious occupation. He had to find some regular source of income and so took the exams to qualify him to teach French in state schools. A post became available in Soria, a sleepy, decrepit provincial capital north-east of Madrid. With a population of only 7,000, the town was growing, owing largely to the extension of the railway line from Torralba. Antonio may not have been greatly inspired to teach, but the landscape captivated him immediately, as the poem *A Orillas del Duero* (Poem IX, pp. 12-13), written in May 1907 on an exploratory visit, demonstrates. Castile, for many of the Generation of '98, was the essential Spain, the stock from which rebirth had to come, a sentiment summed up in Miguel de Unamuno's cry, "¡Gredos, Gredos, Gredos!"[10] Unamuno's ground-breaking essay *Adentro* argued for a subjective, lyrical and philosophical literature. Machado became the poet of the "movement"; he found his individual poetic voice in Castile and acknowledged this by making *Portrait* the first poem in the collection *Campos de Castilla*, "Lands of Castile" (1912), on which his reputation rests.

---

9   Rubén Darío, *Antología Poética*, Prólogo y selección de Guillermo de la Torre (Buenos Aires: Losada, 1973), pp. 165-6.
10   The reference is to the Sierra de Gredos, which runs east-west, lying to the west of Madrid and the south of Avila. Extremely wild and rugged and with a highest peak (Almanzor) of over 8,000 feet, it forms an effective boundary between Old Castile and the present province of Extremadura.

3. *left*: Leonor just before her wedding to Antonio, July 1909.
4. *right*: Leonor and Antonio: wedding photograph, 30 July 1909.

Soria was also indelibly associated with his first great love. When the first *pensión* in which he lodged closed in December 1907, he took a room in another, run by his first landlady's sister, who was married to a retired rural police sergeant named Izquierdo. The elder daughter of the house, Leonor, not quite fourteen when Machado first arrived in Soria, returned from a stay with relatives. Machado, then aged thirty-two, fell in love with her. She returned his love; he discreetly moved out of the house once they became engaged. They were married two years later, on 30 July 1909, when she was just sixteen and he was almost thirty-four. (The age difference would not have seemed as marked as it would now. Men tended to marry later and Leonor was well above the age of consent. It certainly caused no adverse comment in the Machado family, who might have felt that the class difference was more significant, but they were prepared to overlook this and be glad that Antonio had eventually found such happiness.[11]) For a time the couple lived quietly in Soria, with Antonio teaching, writing for reviews and the local press, and exploring the local countryside and capturing it in verse.

---

11   Information from Doña Mercedes Lecea Machado, granddaughter of Antonio's youngest brother Francisco, based on conversations with her mother.

Late in 1910 he was given a grant to study French philology in Paris. He went there with Leonor in January 1911, and listened to lectures by Henri Bergson as well as studying at the Collège de France. But Leonor was showing the first symptoms of "galloping consumption," and in September they returned to Spain with her seriously ill. She died at ten in the evening on 1 August 1912; they had been married just three years and a day. Antonio summed up these five years in his laconic 1917 Prologue: "In 1907 I obtained a post as French teacher, which I carried out for five years in Soria. There I married; there my wife died. Her memory goes with me everywhere."

Baeza

Campos de Castilla had been published just a week before Leonor's death. Its success saved Machado. He wrote to his friend and fellow-poet Juan Ramón Jiménez: "When I lost my wife I thought of shooting myself. The success of the book saved me and not —God knows!— out of vanity but because I thought that if there was a useful power in me I had no right to destroy it. Now I want to work, humbly, certainly, but effectively, with truth. We have to defend the Spain that is arising, from the dead sea, from the inert and crushing Spain that threatens to drown everything. . . . From these wildernesses you have a panoramic view of Spanish barbarism, and it is terrifying."[12] He had expressed these feelings in poems such as *The Ephemeral Past* and *The Ephemeral Future*" (Poems CXXXI and CXXXV, pp. 77, 79) and in the lengthy ballad, of which he also wrote a prose version, *La tierra de Alvargonzález*.

Work and his feeling of responsibility for Spain kept Machado going, but he could not face staying in Soria. He applied for a transfer and in October 1912 was posted to Baeza, in eastern Andalusia, as head of French at the *Instituto General y Técnico de Baeza*. (An account of his first day there, when he went to introduce himself to the Head of the Institute, relates that he was met by the beadle, who told him, "The Director is in *la agonía* [death throes]." Machado's expression of concern elicited the explanation that he was in the town casino, popularly known as *La Agonía* because most of its regulars were farmers, who — as everywhere— were constantly moaning about the weather and their crops.[13]) His mother went with him but was able to stay for a few months only. Machado taught and wrote poems, including some short and poignant memories of Leonor (Poems CXIX, CXXI, CXXII and CXXIII, pp. 66-69). He also began to read philosophy, which developed into a consuming interest over the

---

12   Machado, letter to Juan Ramón Jiménez, 1912, in José Luis Cano, *Antonio Machado. Antología Poética. Biografía* (Barcelona, Bruguera, 1982), pp. 542-4.
13   This conversation was recorded by José Chamorro in a Jaén "Bulletin of Studies" in 1958 and by José María Moreiro in the Madrid daily *Ya* in 1975. See José Montero Padilla, *Antonio Machado en su geografía* (Segovia, 1995), p. 65, n. 29.

5. *top:* Soria: main doorway of
the Instituto at which Machado
taught.

6. *bottom:* Soria: bust of Antonio
Machado outside the Instituto.

coming years, and in which he took a second degree in 1916. He would walk regularly, the road from Baeza to Úbeda being one of his favourite routes: "my passions are walking and reading." A former pupil provides a vivid description, borne out by photographs, of him "moving forward with somewhat hobbling steps, leaning on a strong rough stick, with big shoes, a long overcoat with astrakhan collar, black suit with white wing collar and thickly knotted black tie, his soft black hat nearly always crooked; sometimes his noble head with tousled hair was uncovered; he was carefully shaven, but his clothes were stained with ash from the inevitable cigarette."[14] His teaching duties were not onerous, with a one-hour class in the mornings only.

On 8 June 1916 a group of literature students from Granada University, led by a personal friend, came to visit Úbeda and Baeza. Antonio read his long ballad *La tierra de Alvargonzález* to them, and one of the students read some of his own poems and played the piano. This was Federico García Lorca, and the meeting started the friendship that was to last until Lorca was killed (see Poem LXXXIV S, pp. 105-107).

The First World War saw Machado siding decisively with the Allies. He wrote articles and signed manifestos. His old master Francisco Giner de los Ríos died in February 1915, which occasioned one of his finest poems as well as an article on him. He contributed frequently to the recently founded review *España*, edited by Ortega y Gasset, and to other literary journals. He continued his long country walks, exploring the source of the Guadalquivir in the Sierra de Cazorla, just as he had earlier explored the source of the Duero in the Sierra de Urbión near Soria. Strikes, demonstrations, and frequent changes of government made this a tense time in Spain, even though the country kept out of the war. Antonio Machado himself took part in a demonstration requesting the release of political prisoners. It was also a time of disputes and tensions among the board of the Institute in Baeza, which distressed him, and in 1919 he decided to look for another post, preferably nearer Madrid.

Segovia and Madrid. "Guiomar"

In November 1919 Antonio Machado began teaching at the *Instituto General y Técnico* in Segovia, where he was to stay for twelve years. After a short stay in a hotel, he found a modest *pensión*, run by Doña Luisa Torrego, where he lodged for twelve years, living in conditions that an impoverished student might cavil at today, but which then were perhaps not so unusual for middle-class Spaniards with no private fortunes.[15] He was welcomed in the local press as "the energetic

14   Rafael Laínez Alcalá, "Recuerdo de Antonio Machado en Baeza (1914-1918)," in Ricardo Gullón and Allen W. Phillips (eds.), *Antonio Machado* (Madrid, 1973), p. 88 (cited in Montero Padilla, *op.cit.*, pp. 69-70).
15   The house was virtually unchanged when Doña Luisa died in the 1970s and has been converted into a museum dedicated to Antonio Machado, with his room furnished

and learned poet . . . who in beautiful verses has sung the beauties of Castile, of which he is a fervent lover."[16] Segovia was close enough to Madrid for Machado to spend every weekend there, and he began to take a prominent part in the literary and theatrical life of the capital. He became involved in the creation of the Popular University of Segovia, a non-State body designed to provide courses and lectures for working people. He continued writing for reviews and papers, including *Índice*, founded the previous year by Juan Ramón Jiménez, and he renewed his contacts with Soria by writing for its daily paper. In 1923 Ortega y Gasset started the *Revista de Occidente*, and Machado contributed to it from the first issue. His collection of poems titled *Nuevas canciones* was published in 1924, and in 1925 he was made a corresponding member of the Hispanic Society of America and was a member of the jury for the National Literature Prize. He was a regular member of Madrid's literary *tertulias*, informal gatherings held at cafés such as the Pombo or the Gijón, Machado's favourite, where the dramatist Ramón del Valle Inclán described him, "dressed in his notary's black suit, silent and withdrawn, as sweet and austere as an old Spanish tree."[17] There were similar gatherings in Segovia, and he gradually collected a circle of close friends in the town, including the potter Fernando Arranz and the painter Ignacio Zuloaga. Among these, "the noble figure of Machado —admirable even in his usual unkempt state— spread around him an atmosphere of serene goodness, of affable simplicity":[18] "In the best sense of the word, good," as he had written in his *Portrait* of himself (Poem XCVII, p. 45).

He was also writing plays in collaboration with his brother Manuel: *Las desdichas de la fortuna o Julianillo Valcárcel* was put on by the María Guerrero Company at the Princesa Theatre in 1926 (and at the Juan Bravo in Segovia in December 1928); *Juan de Mañara* at the Reina Victoria the following year; and *Las adelfas* at the Centro the year after that. In 1927 Antonio Machado was made a member of the Royal Language Academy (though he never completed or delivered his inaugural speech). In 1927 (or possibly 1928) he fell in love for the second and last time in his life. The object of his love, addressed as "Guiomar" in his poems (the name of his beloved Jorge Manrique's wife: see Poem LVIII, pp. 26-27), was also a poet, and married. Her name was Pilar de Valderrama, and they saw each other regularly until they were separated by the Civil War. (Their

---

as he left it in 1932. He had to go through another lodger's room from the dining room in order to reach his. The house is just down a steep hill from the convent of the Discalced Carmelites, and the balcony of his room now overlooks a modern statue of a great sixteenth-century poet, St John of the Cross, shown striding purposefully towards the house, suggesting a meeting "through time" that would certainly have delighted Machado.

16 *El Adelantado de Segovia*, 26 Nov. 1919, cited in Montero Padilla, p.79.

17 P. Laín Entralgo, *La espera y la esperanza: historia y teoría del esperar humano*, (1908; 2d ed. Madrid, Alianza, 1984).

18 Mariano Grau, *Antonio Machado en Segovia* (Segovia 1968), p. 33.

affair shocked the family far more than the age and class differences between him and Leonor.) More plays by the two brothers appeared: *La Lola se va a los puertos* in 1929; *La prima Fernanda* in 1931; *La duquesa de Benamejí* in 1932.

Antonio took an active part in supporting the Second Republic. On 14 February 1931, in the Teatro Juan Bravo, he introduced three eminent speakers who had recently signed the influential "Association in the Service of the Republic": Gregorio Marañón, José Ortega y Gasset, and Ramón Pérez de Ayala. A photograph shows the four waiting in the wings of the theatre.[19] *La prima Fernanda* opened at the Juan Bravo just ten days after the proclamation of the Republic in April, when Antonio and a few others raised the Republican flag in Segovia. A letter to Guiomar, however, suggests a more detached attitude: "Those of us charged with keeping order and carrying on the internal government of the city were a few Platonic republicans. That is the sum total of your poet's involvement in the new regime, from which I shall remain as far distant as from the previous one."[20]

He left Segovia in 1932 and moved to Madrid, teaching at the new *Instituto Calderón de la Barca* and living with the family of his younger brother José, who always treated him with immense respect, affection, and patience. The last quality was needed: Antonio made José walk each evening to the end of the Paseo de la Castellana and back, the outward part in total silence; as soon as they turned, he would start talking. Antonio found it difficult to work in a house full of children and, ever given to insomnia and working at night, would march to the bathroom every so often, dip his head in cold water, and come back shaking the water off his hair down the corridor.[21]

In October, twenty years after the publication of *Campos de Castilla*, he was made an "adoptive son" of Soria by the Town Council, "for having been able to describe the landscape, customs and soul of Soria in sublime verses." In his letter of acceptance he wrote that he was indebted to Soria for "learning there to feel Castile, which is the shortest and best way to feeling Spain."

His fictional *alter ego* Juan de Mairena began signing a regular column in the *Diario de Madrid* in 1934, commenting on social, cultural, and political affairs from a committed liberal standpoint. The following year Machado moved to the *Instituto Lope de Vega* and became a member of the "Association of Writers for the Defence of Freedom." Early in 1936 he was the spokesman for the Spanish Committee of the Universal Peace Union. In July the Spanish Civil War broke out, and in August Federico García Lorca was assassinated (see Poem

---

19 A print of this hangs in the bar of the Parador Nacional Antònio Machado in Soria. It is reproduced on p. 125 of Montero Padilla (note 13 above). Machado had known Ortega y Gasset and Pérez de Ayala previously, but this was the only time he met Marañón (information from his grandson, Tom Burns Marañón).

20 Concha Espina, *De Antonio Machado a su grande y secreto amor* (Madrid, 1950), p. 109.

21 Family memories, passed on by Doña Mercedes Lecea Machado.

7. *top:* Segovia. House in the Calle de Desamparados in which Machado lodged.
8. *bottom:* Segovia. Machado's bedroom.

LXXXIVS, pp. 105-107). Machado's *Poesías completas* went into a fourth edition, but the war quickly brought an end to normal literary life in Madrid. Valuing his voice, in November 1936 the Republican government insisted that he and José's family move to the (then) relative safety of Valencia.

Flight to France and death

After spending a short time in the *Casa de Cultura* in Valencia itself, Antonio, his mother, brothers, and nieces found a house in the nearby small town of Rocafort. 1937 passed in relative tranquility; Antonio published his last book, *La Guerra*, prose pieces and a few poems, with illustrations by José. He took a prominent part in the Second International Writers' Conference, held in Valencia and Madrid, then still in government hands, delivering a speech on "The defence and diffusion of culture." The situation worsened, and in April 1938 the family was moved by the government authorities to Barcelona, which was rapidly filling up with refugees fleeing from Franco's advancing troops. They were originally lodged in the Hotel Majestic, then in a mansion called Torre del Castañar. Apparently luxurious, this was filled with refugees, and the comfort was more apparent than real. Antonio wrote for the two main daily papers, following his usual habit of working most, if not all, of the night. By the end of the year it was becoming clear that prominent Republican intellectuals were not going to survive the imminent Nationalist victory. The university governing body arranged for the Machado family and a few friends to join the exodus to France in the night of 22-23 January 1939. After being driven to Cerviá del Ter, where they spent three days, they had to walk to the outskirts of Figueras, where Antonio and his mother spent their last night in Spain, that of 26-27 January. The next day, after a terrible journey and chaos at the border with France, which had officially closed its borders to refugees the previous year, a friend told a police officer that Machado was the Spanish equivalent of Paul Valéry. The policeman must have been a person of some culture, as he lent his car to take the family to the station at Cerbère, where they spent the night in a railway coach in a siding. The next day, though hardly able to walk, they found rooms in the hotel Bougnol Quintana in Collioure, on the coast about ten miles from the border.

Depressed and frail, Antonio left the hotel only once, on 17 February, when, with his brother José, he struggled to the beach to see the sea. The next day he fell gravely ill, with gastro-enteritis added to his chronic bronchitis ("the inevitable cigarette") and weak heart. He died in the hotel on 22 February. The last photograph taken of him alive shows the ravages of the journey all too clearly. His last words were a farewell to his mother, "Adiós, madre." There is another photograph of him on his death-bed, draped in the Republican flag by friends. His mother died three days later, and they were buried side-by-side in a tomb belonging to friends of the hotel landlady in the town cemetery. Their bodies remain there to this day. His death had turned the last stanza of his *Portrait* into a terrible prophecy (see Poem XCVII, p. 45).

9. *left:* The last photograph of Machado alive: Collioure, Feb. 1939.
10. *right:* Street named after Machado in Collioure.

Machado's Works
SOLEDADES

The title of Machado's first collection, *Soledades*, indicates the extent to which he was at the time immersed in his own thoughts and isolation. He is alone, and in his loneliness he dreams. In his dreams he evokes the past, transported to the present through the image of water, water in springs, fountains, and rivers. Its endless rhythms and patterns of sound are heard within him while at the same time they reflect the passage of his life. Children's voices remind him of his own voice and join with his to form part of the eternal flow of water: "I listen to the songs/with their ancient rhythms/the children are singing. . . ." (Poem VIII, p. 11).

An enlarged collection was published in 1907, with the title expanded to *Soledades, galerías y otros poemas.* The new poems dealt with much the same themes, adding the metaphor of the long gallery, down which the poet looks back and forward over his life, contemplating his loneliness in dreams. The tone is deeply introspective and the form post-Symbolist. There are musical effects reminiscent of Darío's Modernism, with echoes of Verlaine in the rhythm and the sound. Machado was formally appointed to his teaching post in Soria on 7 May the same year, 1907, though he did not move there to start teaching until the autumn, at the start of the academic year 1907-8. He found himself physically even more alone. He sought solace in the townscape and the surrounding landscape, taking late night walks through the deserted streets: "Cold Soria! The courthouse/clock strikes one" (Poem CXIII, *Around Soria* VI, p. 59). Lonely he may be, but in his loneliness he now starts to focus on factors outside himself —the land of Castile, which brings with it the essential, and essentially tragic, past of Spain.

CAMPOS DE CASTILLA

Campos de Castilla was published in 1912. It therefore covers the five years that included his marriage to Leonor, their time in Paris, and her illness and death. The collection starts, by way of a preface, with *Portrait* (Poem XCVII, p. 47) written in 1906, which sets his past self in relation to his present and his future. His memories of his native Seville and the Madrid of his schooldays, together with his reading —Classical, Romantic, Modernist, and going back to Ronsard— have brought him to the point where he can express what he now is through what he sees and what he feels about what he sees. The following year he found the deepest source of the emotion felt: the landscape of Castile. The emotion is carried by simple observation; there is no need for self-analysis and again no anecdote:[22] "The Duero crosses the oaken heart/of Iberia and Castile" (Poem XCVIII, p. 49). These are words that both express an ongoing reality and define a moment in time: the poet observing. Machado has become what Pedro Laín Entralgo has called "the poet of personal time." He has moved on from the Bergsonian dialogue with his inner self —*Ese Bergson es un tuno. ¿Verdad, Maestro Unamuno?* ("That Bergson's a rogue, isn't he, master Unamuno?") He deliberately refers this new objectivity to Unamuno, the guiding spirit of the Generation of '98. Unamuno was also one of the first to recognize the importance of *Campos de Castilla*, in a letter to the Madrid daily *ABC*. Machado himself came relatively late to the spirit of the "movement" —if it can be called such— but became one of its most expressive voices. "Then his poetry takes on an epic twist, becomes the mouthpiece of the society to which it belongs, and tries to be its collective memory."[23] "On the banks of the Duero" (Poem

---

22   See the note to Poem VIII, p. 109.
23   Manuel Alvar, introduction to *Poesías completas* (31st ed., Madrid 2000), p. 26. This latest edition, with a long introduction (to which this section is heavily indebted),

XCVIII, p. 47), written in response to his earlier visit to Soria in spring 1907, was added to the expanded version of *Soledades*, published at the end of that year. It stands out as Machado's first "Generation of '98" poem in an otherwise Romantic book.[24]

Antonio had been able to put a copy of his masterpiece into Leonor's hands just a week before her death. It had been officially published in June, but his author's copies did not reach him till 24 July. A series of nine new poems referring to her death was added to later editions (from 1917). They express his devastation, but move from there to resignation—"Now, Lord, we're alone—my heart and the sea" (Poem CXIX, p. 67)—and to a form of hope. The landscape, charged with the historical tragedy of Spain, is now charged with his personal tragedy as well. Leonor's grave, which he asks his friend José María Palacio, a journalist from Soria, to visit in spring (Poem CXXVI, p. 71) is her *tierra*, the very soil, earth, ground, land (the Spanish word meaning any or all of these) of Castile. He has a further motive for feeling "sorrow, sorrow that is love" for the lands of Soria, now carried with him in memory to Baeza. But Soria could not represent only the past and sorrow: it was also the way to the heart of Spain.

Machado took his concern for Spain to Baeza. He wrote to Juan Ramón Jiménez, in the letter already cited, "I believe that conquest of the future can be achieved only through a sum of qualities. Otherwise the mass will swamp us. If we do not form a single vital and rushing current the Spanish inertia will triumph. [. . .] At times the problem of our country concerns me passionately. . . But nothing immediate and direct can be done. There's an atmosphere of cowardice and lies that chokes one. It's really iniquitous how we have made a tacit agreement to respect everything hollow and fictitious and to disdain what's real. It seems as though we are all thinking, with deep conviction, that there is one thing sacred: lies." This is the frame of mind that produced *The Ephemeral Past* and *The Ephemeral Future* (Poems CXXXI and CXXXV, p. 77, 79). "And when it comes to the religious question, above all, the Spanish soul sounds like papier mâché" (see Poem CXXX, *La saeta*, p. 75). Work has to go on, despite his personal loss: "We have to defend the Spain that is arising. . . ." He was to give succinct expression to this determination two-and-a-half years later in the poem dedicated to his former master, Francisco Giner de los Ríos, who died on 17 February 1915: "Let anvils ring and bells be silent!" (The poem was completed four days later; see Poem CXXXIX, p. 85). This was a call to him, too, to move forward, on from the Generation of '98, on from the landscape of Castile, on from memories of death, to look for a new poetic voice.

---

and a "reading workshop" at the end, runs to well over 500 pages, as opposed to the 270 of the original (Buenos Aires, 1943) edition, evidence of the number of poems discovered since this. The 2000 edition claims to be the first that is truly complete.

24   Alvar, p. 29, citing Gregorio Salvador, *"Orillas del Duero", de Antonio Machado* (2d ed., Madrid, 1973).

NUEVAS CANCIONES Y OBRAS POSTERIORES

Some fifty short aphorisms and other pieces, grouped under the number CXXXVI and included, somewhat incongruously, in later editions of *Campos de Castilla*, are an indication of a new poetic direction. Machado had always had a deep feeling for popular verse, inherited largely perhaps from his father, who had been a distinguished collector of *flamenco* songs. Antonio had planned to write a modern *Romancero*, a collection of ballads to rival those from the fourteenth to sixteenth centuries, but the verse version of *La tierra de Alvargonzález* was all he managed to produce. In Baeza he looked at the landscape once more, as he had in Soria, but recorded it in popular terms and rhythms, lacking the personal emotion of his poems of Castile.

He also turned to reading philosophy, from the ancients Plato, Pythagoras, and Aristotle to Descartes, Leibnitz, Schopenhauer, Nietzsche and Heidegger. He wrestled with human relationship to God, but lacked the rooted faith of a St Augustine or St John of the Cross in a God who was both living and life-giving: "Machado could not reach sufficient certainty about the relationship between his heart and God" (Laín Entralgo). And God was divided into the God of Spain's past, "nailed to wood," the God of the "faith of my elders," and the "one who walked on the sea," the God he was looking for (see Poem CXXX *La saeta*, p. 77). He doubted his own worth, the meaning of life, the process of time, the existence of God: without God the *"Nada, nada, nada, nada"* —the "nothingness" faced by St John of the Cross (who had died in Úbeda)— was more frightening still. Machado turned more philosopher than poet. His voice is full of resignation rather than despair in the face of these mysteries; it is existentialist, but not darkly so.

In Heidegger, whom he read in a French translation, he found the individual ineluctably faced with his own finitude, human existence inescapably bound by the horizon of its own meaning, as being-for-death. This is the real and original feature of being human: death, its uncertainty, and the loneliness with which we have to face it. But what appealed most to Machado in Heidegger was that he looked for the ultimate meaning of human life not through great minds but through the most "ordinary" people. This linked his own philosophy with his growing use of a deliberately popular voice in his poetry. It found an echo in his fictional philosopher *alter ego*, Juan de Mairena, whose apocryphal portrait of his "master," the equally fictitious Abél Martín, applies aptly to his real creator:

My master loved the old Spanish cities, whose deserted streets he liked to walk in the small hours of the morning, disturbing the peace of the cats, who fled in terror at his approach. Nevertheless, he was such a naturally sociable man that he rarely returned to his lodging without engaging the night-watchman of his quarter in conversation.

"Nothing going on here, then?"

"The cats and you."

"And that cloak you're wearing, does it keep you warm enough?"

"Well enough, Sir."

"But when the nights are really cold?"

"I go into that doorway and huddle up in there, well wrapped-up, with my lantern between my legs. "

"You mean, the lantern warms you?"

I'll say!

"You're a true philosopher."

"Life teaches one a lot."

"Good night." `

"Good night." (From *Juan de Mairena*, XLVI)

Machado's creation of other characters, whom he makes to converse on the meaning of life, can be seen as an expression of his own uncertainties. Their first appearance was in 1931 in *Cancionero apócrifo de Abél Martín*, which includes brief notes on "twelve poets who might have existed" —actually seventeen— followed in most cases by examples of their verse. They include an Antonio Machado "not to be confused with the famous author of *Soledades* and *Campos de Castilla*." *Juan de Mairena. Sentencias, donaires, apuntes y recuerdos de un profesor apócrifo* followed in 1936. In the manner of Socrates, the apocryphal characters discuss a series of human problems, including the emotional and intellectual problems involved in being a poet. Martín, the teacher, who reads Leibnitz and is atheist and a bachelor, and Mairena, his pupil, are aspects of the more complex, mature Machado (the fact that all three names begin with M is perhaps deliberate). Whimsy, alienation, perhaps post-modernism *ante diem*? Machado the poet was keeping his lyrical voice to himself yet had other things to say and so devised other voices in which to say them.

With the fall of the monarchy in 1930 and the proclamation of the Second Republic the following year, Machado (aided, perhaps, by his new emotional involvement with "Guiomar") felt more committed to society and to intellectual and political life. He spoke often in public and wrote extensively for the press; during the Civil War he was the mainstay of the review *Hora de España*, contributing a prose article and sometimes a poem to every issue during its two-year existence. He expressed his concern for the hardships borne by peasants in the country and for the republican forces facing a constantly deteriorating situation. He was facing up to "otherness" —in himself, in other people, in the world around him. In the few "Poems of War" anecdote —banished from his poetry from *Soledades* onward— makes an appearance as he engages with the sufferings of others: "The mother by the bedside/squeezes his little hand" . . . (*The Death of the Wounded Child*, Poem LXXVI S, p. 103). He became ever more conscious of the inexorable march of time, hearing "twelve-year-old/voices in his fifty-year-old ears" (*The Death of Abél Martín*, Poem CLXX, p. 99), and confronted by the prospect of *Nada*: "Oh, deep wisdom of the zero, savour/of mature fruit for man alone to taste" (*ibid.*, p. 113). Here, and also in the sonnet *Al gran cero* and *In Memory of Abél Martín* (Poem CLXX, p. 103), he is expressing his final metaphysical understanding: God "the Being who is . . . can only create what is other than himself: Not-Being. Human consciousness . . . recoils upon the knowledge of its own limits, its frontiers with [not-being, death] etc.: and so discursive thought is born. The concept of Not-Being, with its child, Thought, belongs to man"[25]—so "fruit for man alone to taste." At the very end, though, stripped of everything, metaphysic gives way to the old assertive manner in Antonio's last line of verse, found by his brother José in his coat pocket after his death:

Estos días azules y este sol de la infancia.
These blue days and this childhood sun.

25 J. B. Trend, note to sonnet *Al gran cero*, in *The Oxford Book of Spanish Verse* (2d ed., Oxford, 1940), p. 502.

11. *"Shepherds with their long cloaks"*
(See Poem CXXVI *To José María Palacio*, p. 73)

Solitudes
(1899-1907)

Soledades

I
EL VIAJERO

Está en la sala familiar, sombría,
y entre nosotros, el querido hermano
que en el sueño infantil de un claro día
vimos partir hacia un país lejano.
Hoy tiene ya las sienes plateadas,
un gris mechón sobre la angosta frente;
y la fría inquietud de sus miradas
revela un alma casi toda ausente.
Deshójanse las copas otoñales
del parque mustio y viejo.
La tarde, tras los húmedos cristales,
se pinta, y en el fondo del espejo.
El rostro del hermano se ilumina
suavemente: ¿Floridos desengaños
dorados por la tarde que declina?
¿Ansias de vida nueva en nuevos años?
¿Lamentará la juventud perdida?
Lejos quedó —la pobre loba— muerta.
¿La blanca juventud nunca vivida
teme, que ha de cantar ante su puerta?
¿Sonríe al sol de oro
de la tierra de un sueño no encontrada;
y ve su nave hender el mar sonoro,
de viento y luz la blanca vela hinchada?
Él ha visto las hojas otoñales,
amarillas, rodar, las olorosas
ramas del eucalipto, los rosales
que enseñan otra vez sus blancas rosas . . .

I

THE TRAVELLER[1]

Back with us now, in the shadowy
living room, is the dear brother
whom we saw leave for a distant land
in the childish dreams of a sunlit day.
    His temples now are flecked with silver,
and a grey lock falls on his narrow brow,
while the cold anxiety of his gaze
shows a virtually absent soul.
    The autumn leaves are falling
from tree-tops in the musty old park.
Evening, behind misted window panes,
is painted too in the mirror's depths.
    Gradually, our brother's face
lightens. Florid disappointments
gilded by the fading light?
Longings for a new life yet to come?
    Is he lamenting his lost youth,
dead—poor she-wolf—in foreign parts?
Or does he fear youth, fair, unlived,
that will one day sing at his door?
    Is he smiling at the golden sun
of an unfound land in his dreams
and seeing his ship cleave the sounding sea,
its white sail filled with wind and light?
    He has seen the yellow leaves
of autumn swirl around, the scented
eucalyptus branches, rose bushes
show their white blooms once again . . .

Y este dolor que añora o desconfía
el temblor de una lágrima reprime,
y un resto de viril hipocresía
en el semblante pálido se imprime.
    Serio retrato en la pared clarea
todavía. Nosotros divagamos.
En la tristeza del hogar golpea
el tictac del reloj. Todos callamos.

II

He andado muchos caminos,
he abierto muchas veredas;
he navegado en cien mares,
y atracado en cien riberas.
    En todas partes he visto
caravanas de tristeza,
soberbios y melancólicos
borrachos de sombra negra,
    y pedantones al paño
que miran, callan, y piensan
que saben, porque no beben
el vino de las tabernas.
    Mala gente que camina
y va apestando la tierra . . .
    Y en todas partes he visto
gentes que danzan o juegan,
cuando pueden, y laboran
sus cuatro palmos de tierra.

And this nostalgia or suspicious pain
holds back a trembling tear,
while a last trace of manly hypocrisy
is imprinted on his pale face.
A stern portrait on the wall still
reflects the light. Thoughts wander.
The clock ticks on in the dreary
house. We are all silent.

II

I have walked down many roads
and trodden many paths;
I have sailed a hundred seas
and moored on a hundred shores.
Everywhere, I have seen
caravans of sadness,
proud and melancholic
drunks with black shadows,
and great pedants in the wings
watching, silent, thinking
they know better for not drinking
the wine of the taverns.
Bad people going about
polluting the earth . . .
And everywhere, I have seen
people who dance or play
when they can, and who work
their own small plots of land.

Nunca, si llegan a un sitio,
preguntan a dónde llegan.
Cuando caminan, cabalgan
a lomos de mula vieja,
y no conocen la prisa
ni aun en los días de fiesta.
Donde hay vino, beben vino;
donde no hay vino, agua fresca.
Son buenas gentes que viven,
laboran, pasan y sueñan,
y en un día como tantos
descansan bajo la tierra.

III

La plaza y los naranjos encendidos
con sus frutas redondas y risueñas.
Tumulto de pequeños colegiales
que, al salir en desorden de la escuela,
llenan el aire de la plaza en sombra
con la algazara de sus voces nuevas.
¡Alegría infantil en los rincones
de las ciudades muertas! . . .
¡Y algo nuestro de ayer, que todavía
vemos vagar por estas calles viejas!

If they arrive somewhere
they never ask where they are;
when they travel, they ride
on the backs of ancient mules,
    and they are never hurried—
not even on feast-days.
Where there's wine, they drink it;
where there's none, cold water.
    They are good people who live,
work, move on, and dream;
and on a day just like so many,
they rest beneath the earth.

III

The square and its orangetrees alight
with their round and cheerful fruit.
    Uproar of little children
tumbling out of school,
filling the air of the shady square
with the riot of their fresh voices.
    Youthful joy in the crannies
of crumbling cities! . . .
And something of our past that we still see
wandering these old streets!

IV
EN EL ENTIERRO DE UN AMIGO

Tierra le dieron una tarde horrible
del mes de julio, bajo el sol de fuego.
    A un paso de la abierta sepultura,
había rosas de podridos pétalos,
entre geranios de áspera fragancia
y roja flor. El cielo
puro y azul. Corría
un aire fuerte y seco.
    De los gruesos cordeles suspendido,
pesadamente, descender hicieron
el ataúd al fondo de la fosa
los dos sepultureros . . .
    Y al reposar sonó con recio golpe,
solemne, en el silencio.
    Un golpe de ataúd en tierra es algo
perfectamente serio.
    Sobre la negra caja se rompían
los pesados terrones polvorientos . . .
    El aire se llevaba
de la honda fosa el blanquecino aliento.
    —Y tú, sin sombra ya, duerme y reposa,
larga paz a tus huesos . . .
    Definitivamente,
duerme un sueño tranquilo y verdadero.

IV
AT THE BURIAL OF A FRIEND

They buried him one brutal afternoon
in the month of July, under the burning sun.
   Close by the open grave
were roses with rotting petals
among sour-smelling geraniums
with red flowers. The sky
clear and blue. A strong
dry wind was blowing.
   Hanging heavy from thick ropes,
the coffin was eased down
to the bottom of the pit
by two gravediggers . . .
   When it touched ground it sounded
a solid, solemn thud in the silence.
   The thud of a coffin on the ground
is a totally serious thing.
   Heavy clods of dusty earth
broke on the black box . . .
   The wind carried bleached breath
from the depth of the pit.
   —And you, now shadowless, sleep and repose:
may your bones long rest in peace. . . .
   Until the end of time,
sleep a true and tranquil dream.

VIII

Yo escucho los cantos
de viejas cadencias
que los niños cantan
cuando en coro juegan
y vierten en coro
sus almas que sueñan,
cual vierten sus aguas
las fuentes de piedra:
con monotonías
de risas eternas
que no son alegres,
con lágrimas viejas
que no son amargas,
y dicen tristezas,
tristezas de amores
de antiguas leyendas.
  En los labios niños
las canciones llevan
confusa la historia
y clara la pena;
como clara el agua
lleva su conseja
de viejos amores
que nunca se cuentan.
  Jugando, a la sombra
de una plaza vieja,
los niños cantaban . . .
  La fuente de piedra
vertía su eterno
cristal de leyenda.
  Cantaban los niños
canciones ingenuas,
de un algo que pasa
y que nunca llega:

VIII[2]

I listen to the songs
with ancient rhythms
the children are singing
as they play ring o' roses,
pouring out in chorus
their dreaming souls,
like stone fountains
pouring out their waters:
with changeless cadences
of ageless laughter,
not truly joyful,
with ancient tears
not truly bitter,
telling of sadness,
the sadness of loves
in ancient legends.
  On childish lips
the songs deliver
a muddled story
and a clear pain;
as the clear water
carries its fable
of ancient loves
that are never told.
  Playing, in the shade
of an ancient square,
the children were chanting. . . .
The fountain of stone
poured out its eternal
clear flow of tales.
  The children were chanting
their simple refrain
of something that passes
and never arrives:

la historia confusa
y clara la pena.
Seguía su cuento
la fuente serena;
borrada la historia,
contaba la pena.

IX
ORILLAS DEL DUERO

Se ha asomado una cigüeña a lo alto del campanario.
Girando en torno a la torre y al caserón solitario,
ya las golondrinas chillan. Pasaron del blanco invierno,
de nevascas y ventiscas los crudos soplos de infierno.
Es una tibia mañana.
El sol calienta un poquito la pobre tierra soriana.
Pasados los verdes pinos,
casi azules, primavera
se ve brotar en los finos
chopos de la carretera
y del río. El Duero corre, terso y mudo, mansamente.
El campo parece, más que joven, adolescente.
Entre las hierbas alguna humilde flor ha nacido,
azul o blanca. ¡Belleza del campo apenas florido,
y mística primavera!
¡Chopos del camino blanco, álamos de la ribera,
espuma de la montaña
ante la azul lejanía,
sol del día, claro día!
¡Hermosa tierra de España!

a muddled story
with a clear pain.
   Calmly, the fountain
went on with its tale—
no trace of the story,
just the clear pain.

IX
BANKS OF THE DUERO

A stork has appeared on top of the bell tower.
Wheeling round the tower and the lone old
farmhouse, swallows cry. White winter's harsh
hell-breaths of snow-flurry and storm are gone.
   It is a mild morning.
The sun faintly warms the poor earth of Soria.
   Beyond the green pines, verging on
blue, spring is breaking out
in the narrow poplars[3] by the road and
the river. The Duero flows gently, taut and dumb.
The land, if not young, looks youthful.
   Among the grasses common flowers
show white or blue. Burgeoning beauty,
mystical spring!
   Poplars by the white track, poplars on the bank,
the mountain foaming
against the blue distance
of a sunlit day, bright day!
Beautiful land of Spain!

XI

Yo voy soñando caminos
de la tarde. ¡Las colinas
doradas, los verdes pinos,
las polvorientas encinas!...
¿Adónde el camino irá?
Yo voy cantando, viajero
a lo largo del sendero...
—La tarde cayendo está—.
"En el corazón tenía
la espina de una pasión;
logré arrancármela un día:
ya no siento el corazón."
Y todo el campo un momento
se queda, mudo y sombrío,
meditando. Suena el viento
en los álamos del río.
La tarde más se oscurece;
y el camino que serpea
y débilmente blanquea,
se enturbia y desaparece.
Mi cantar vuelve a plañir:
"Aguda espina dorada,
quién te pudiera sentir
en el corazón clavada."

XI

I walk along dreaming
of roads in the evening—
golden hills, green pines,
dust-covered ilexes!
Where will the road lead?
I sing as I travel
the whole length of the path,
with evening now falling:
"Once I had the thorn
of a passion in my heart;
one day I plucked it forth—
now I can't feel my heart."
  And the whole countryside
is suddenly quiet and dark,
meditating. The wind rustles
in the poplars by the river.
  The evening grows darker still,
and the feeble pale gleam
of the winding road
becomes cloudy and fades.
  My song once more mourns:
"Sharp golden thorn,
would I could feel you
fixed in my heart."

XIV
CANTE HONDO

Yo meditaba absorto, devanando
los hilos del hastío y la tristeza,
cuando llegó a mi oído,
por la ventana de mi estancia, abierta
    a una caliente noche de verano,
el plañir de una copla soñolienta,
quebrada por los trémolos sombríos
de las músicas magas de mi tierra.
... Y era el Amor, como una roja llama
—Nerviosa mano en la vibrante cuerda
ponía un largo suspirar de oro
que se trocaba en surtidor de estrellas—.
... Y era la Muerte, al hombro la cuchilla,
el paso largo, torva y esquelética.
—Tal cuando yo era niño la soñaba—.
    Y en la guitarra, resonante y trémula,
la brusca mano, al golpear, fingía
el reposar de un ataúd en tierra.
    Y era un plañido solitario el soplo
que el polvo barre y la ceniza avienta.

XIV
DEEP SONG

Wrapped in myself and thought, I was
unpicking threads of weariness and gloom,
when through the windows of my room,
open to a summer night,
my ears caught the lament
of a dreamy ballad, fractured
by the brooding tremolos
of the magic music of my land.
  And it was Love, like a red flame . . .
A taut hand on the vibrant string
formed a long golden sigh,
which became a spurt of stars.
  And it was Death, scythe on shoulder,
long-leggèd, skeletal, grim,
just as in my childhood dreams.
  And on the guitar, resonant, quivering,
the brusque hand, drumming, made the sound
of a coffin hitting the ground.
  And the lonely lament was a gust
that fans the ashes and scatters the dust.

XXI

Daba el reloj las doce ... y eran doce
golpes de azada en tierra ...
... ¡Mi hora! —grité— El silencio
me respondió: —No temas;
tú no verás caer la última gota
que en la clepsidra tiembla.
    Dormirás muchas horas todavía
sobre la orilla vieja
y encontrarás una mañana pura
amarrada tu barca a otra ribera.

XXXV

Al borde del sendero un día nos sentamos.
Ya nuestra vida es tiempo, y nuestra sola cuita
son las desesperantes posturas que tomamos
para aguardar ... Mas Ella no faltará a la cita.

XXI

The clock struck twelve . . . twelve strokes
of the pick's hollow thuds on the earth.
   "My time!" I cried. Silence
answered me: "Fear not;
you will not see the last drop
fall trembling from the water-clock.
   You will sleep many hours yet
on the old shore, then
you will find, one clear morning,
your boat moored on another bank."

XXXV

We sit down on the edge of the path one day.
Now our life is time, and our only care
is the despondent mood in which we wait . . .
But She will not miss the date.

XLIV

El casco roído y verdoso
del viejo falucho
reposa en la arena . . .
La vela tronchada parece
que aún sueña en el sol y en el mar.
 El mar hierve y canta . . .
El mar es un sueño sonoro
bajo el sol de abril.
 El mar hierve y ríe
con olas azules y espumas de leche y de plata,
el mar hierve y ríe
bajo el cielo azul.
El mar lactescente,
el mar rutilante,
que ríe en sus liras de plata sus risas azules . . .
¡Hierve y ríe el mar! . . .
 El aire parece que duerme encantado
en la fúlgida niebla de sol blanquecino.
La gaviota palpita en el aire dormido, y al lento
volar soñoliento, se aleja y se pierde en la bruma del sol.

XLIV

The corroded mossy hulk
of the old felucca lies
half buried in the sand . . .
Its tattered sail still seems
to dream of sun and sea.
    The sea surges and sings . . .
The sea is a resonant dream
under the April sun.
    The sea surges and laughs
in blue waves and foam of silver and milk;
the sea surges and laughs
under the blue sky.
The milky sea,
the sparkling sea,
that laughs its blue laughter in silver lyres . . .
The sea surges and laughs!
    The air, enchanted, seems to sleep
in the shining mist of a bleached-out sun.
In the sleepy air the gull takes wing, slowly,
drowsily vanishing in the sunlit mist.

XLVI
LA NORIA

La tarde caía
triste y polvorienta.
El agua cantaba
su copla plebeya
en los cangilones
de la noria lenta.
Soñaba la mula
¡pobre mula vieja!
al compás de sombra
que en el agua suena.
La tarde caía
triste y polvorienta.
Yo no sé qué noble,
divino poeta
unió a la amargura
de la eterna rueda
la dulce armonía
del agua que sueña
y vendó tus ojos,
¡pobre mula vieja! . . .
Mas sé que fue un noble,
divino poeta,
corazón maduro
de sombra y de ciencia.

XLVI
THE WATERWHEEL

Evening was falling,
dust-laden and sad.
The water was singing
its rustic rhyme
in the dipping buckets
of the slow waterwheel.[4]
The mule was dreaming—
poor old mule!—
to the shadow's beat
heard in the water.
Evening was falling,
dust-laden and sad.
I wonder what noble
and divine poet
joined the bitterness
of the eternal wheel
to the sweet harmony
of dreaming water
and bandaged your eyes—
poor old mule . . .
I know he was a noble
and divine poet
with a heart seasoned
with shadow and knowledge.

LIV
LOS SUEÑOS MALOS

Está la plaza sombría;
muere el día.
Suenan lejos las campanas.
   De balcones y ventanas
se iluminan las vidrieras,
con reflejos mortecinos,
como huesos blanquecinos
y borrosas calaveras.
   En toda la tarde brilla
una luz de pesadilla.
Está el sol en el ocaso.
Suena el eco de mi paso.
   —¿Eres tú? Ya te esperaba . . .
—No eras tú a quien yo buscaba.

LVI

Sonaba el reloj la una,
dentro de mi cuarto. Era
triste la noche. La luna,
reluciente calavera,
   ya del cenit declinando,
iba del ciprés del huerto
fríamente iluminando
el alto ramaje yerto.
   Por la entreabierta ventana
llegaban a mis oídos
metálicos alaridos
de una música lejana.

LIV
BAD DREAMS

The square is shaded;
the day is dying.
Distant bells toll.
    The balcony and window
panes are gleaming
with deathly reflections
like bleached bones
and blurred skulls.
    A nightmarish light
shines all evening long.
The sun is setting;
I hear my steps echo.
    "Is that you? I was waiting."
"It's not you I came for."

LVI

The clock struck one
inside my room. The night
was gloomy. The moon,
a shining skull,
    now setting from its zenith,
cast a cold light
on the tall, stiff branches
of the cypress in my garden.
    Through the half-open window
metallic shrieks
from some distant music
came to my ears.

Una música tristona,
una mazurca olvidada,
entre inocente y burlona,
mal tañida y mal soplada.
  Y yo sentí el estupor
del alma cuando bosteza
el corazón, la cabeza,
y . . . morirse es lo mejor.

LVIII
GLOSA

Nuestras vidas son los ríos
que van a dar a la mar,
que es el morir. ¡Gran cantar!
  Entre los poetas míos
tiene Manrique un altar.
  Dulce goce de vivir:
mala ciencia del pasar,
ciego huir a la mar.
  Tras el pavor del morir
está el placer de llegar.
  Mas ¿y el horror de volver?
¡Gran pesar!

A somewhat sad music,
a forgotten mazurka,
half simple, half mocking,
badly played, badly sung.
    And I felt the lethargy
of the soul when the heart
yawns, and the head,
and . . . best just to die.

LVIII
GLOSS

Our lives are the rivers
that flow down to the sea,
which is dying. Great lines!
    Among the poets I love,
Manrique[5] is sacrosanct.
    Sweet joy of living:
hard knowledge of passing,
fleeing blind to the sea.
    After the terror of dying
comes the joy of arriving.
    Great gladness!
But—the dread of returning?
Great sadness!

LIX

Anoche cuando dormía
soñé, ¡bendita ilusión!,
que una fontana fluía
dentro de mi corazón.
Dí, ¿por qué acequia escondida,
agua, vienes hasta mí,
manantial de nueva vida
en donde nunca bebí?
　Anoche cuando dormía
soñé, ¡bendita ilusión!,
que una colmena tenía
dentro de mi corazón;
y las doradas abejas
iban fabricando en él,
con las amarguras viejas,
blanca cera y dulce miel.
　Anoche cuando dormía
soñé, ¡bendita ilusión!,
que un ardiente sol lucía
dentro de mi corazón.
Era ardiente porque daba
calores de rojo hogar,
y era sol porque alumbraba
y porque hacía llorar.
　Anoche cuando dormía
soñé, ¡bendita ilusión!,
que era Dios lo que tenía
dentro de mi corazón.

LIX

Last night, as I slept,
I dreamt—blest illusion!—
that a spring was flowing
within my heart.
Say, water: what hidden course
brings you to me,
source of our life
never tasted by me?
   Last night, as I slept,
I dreamt—blest illusion!—
that a hive was humming
within my heart;
and the golden bees
were working there turning
my ancient heartaches
to white combs and sweet honey.
   Last night, as I slept,
I dreamt—blest illusion!—
that a strong sun was shining
within my heart—
strong because it warmed me
like coals in the hearth;
sun because it gave me light
and made me weep.
   Last night, as I slept,
I dreamt—blest illusion!—
that it was God I was holding
within my heart.

LXII

Desgarrada la nube; el arco iris
brillando ya en el cielo,
y en un fanal de lluvia
y sol el campo envuelto.
Desperté. ¿Quién enturbia
los mágicos cristales de mi sueño?
Mi corazón latía
atónito y disperso.
. . . ¡El limonar florido,
el cipresal del huerto,
el prado verde, el sol, el agua, el iris! . . .
¡el agua en tus cabellos! . . .
Y todo en la memoria se perdía
como una pompa de jabón al viento.

LXIV

Desde el umbral de un sueño me llamaron . . .
Era la buena voz, la voz querida.
—Dime: ¿vendrás conmigo a ver el alma? . . .
Llegó a mi corazón una caricia.
—Contigo siempre . . . Y avancé en mi sueño
por una larga, escueta galería,
sintiendo el roce de la veste pura
y el palpitar suave de la mano amiga.

LXII

A rent in the cloud; the rainbow's arc
already shining in the sky,
a screen of rain and sunlight
sweeping over the land.
    I awoke. Who is misting
the magical panes of my dream?
My heart went on beating,
astonished and scattered.
    The lemon trees in bloom,
the garden's cypress grove,
green meadow, sun, water, rainbow!
Raindrops in your hair!
    And everything in my memory faded
like a soap bubble cast to the wind.

LXIV

I was summoned from the threshold of a dream . . .
It was the good voice, the beloved voice.
    "Tell me: will you come with me to visit the soul?"
A caress stole into my heart.
    "With you for ever . . . " And I moved on in my dream
down an endless echoing gallery,
feeling the brush of the pure garment
and the gentle pulse of the friendly hand.

LXVIII

Llamó a mi corazón, un claro día,
con un perfume de jazmín, el viento.
—A cambio de este aroma,
todo el aroma de tus rosas quiero.
—No tengo rosas; flores
en mi jardín no hay ya; todas han muerto.
—Me llevaré los llantos de las fuentes,
las hojas amarillas y los mustios pétalos.
Y el viento huyó . . . Mi corazón sangraba . . .
Alma, ¿qué has hecho de tu pobre huerto?

LXX

Y nada importa ya que el vino de oro
rebose de tu copa cristalina,
o el agrio zumo enturbie el puro vaso . . .
    Tú sabes las secretas galerías
del alma, los caminos de los sueños,
y la tarde tranquila
donde van a morir . . . Allí te aguardan
    las hadas silenciosas de la vida,
y hacia un jardín de eterna primavera
te llevarán un día.

LXVIII

One fine day, perfumed with jasmine,
the wind summoned my heart.
"In return for this scent
I want all the scent of your roses."
    "I have no roses; there are
no flowers left in my garden; all are dead."
    "Then I shall take the fountains' weeping,
the yellowed leaves and the withered petals."
    And the wind fled . . . and my heart bled . . .
"Soul, what have you done to your poor garden?"

LXX

It no longer matters if the golden wine
should overflow your crystal cup,
or the bitter lees cloud the clear glass . . .
    You know the secret galleries
of the soul, the way of dreams,
and the tranquil evening
in which they will die . . . The silent spirits
    of life await you there;
and one day they will bear you
to a garden of eternal spring.

LXXII

La casa tan querida
donde habitaba ella,
sobre un montón de escombros arruinada
o derruída, enseña
el negro y carcomido
maltrabado esqueleto de madera.
　La luna está vertiendo
su clara luz en sueños que platea
en las ventanas. Mal vestido y triste,
voy caminando por la calle vieja.

LXXVII

Es una tarde cenicienta y mustia,
destartalada, como el alma mía;
y es esta vieja angustia
que habita mi usual hipocondría.
　La causa de esta angustia no consigo
ni vagamente comprender siquiera;
pero recuerdo y, recordando, digo :
–Sí, yo era niño, y tú, mi compañera.

*

Y no es verdad, dolor, yo te conozco,
tú eres nostalgia de la vida buena
y soledad de corazón sombrío,
de barco sin naufragio y sin estrella.

LXXII

The house I loved so much,
in which she lived—
now a great heap of rubble, ruined
or demolished—reveals
its crumbling wooden skeleton,
blackened and worm-eaten.
  The moon beams down
her bright light in dreams that turn
to silver on the windows. Ill clad and sad,
I walk on down the old street.

LXXVII

It is a gloomy, ashen evening,
bedraggled, like my soul;
and I feel the same old anguish—
familiar hypochondria's tenant.
  What causes this anguish I cannot
even vaguely comprehend;
but I think back and recall:
"Yes, I was young, and you were my girl."

*

And it's not true, sorrow—I know you:
you are the longing for the good life
and the loneliness of a darkened heart,
of an unwrecked ship without a star.

Como perro olvidado que no tiene
huella ni olfato y yerra
por los caminos, sin camino, como
el niño que en la noche de una fiesta
    se pierde entre el gentío
y el aire polvoriento y las candelas
chispeantes, atónito, y asombra
su corazón de música y de pena,
    así voy yo, borracho melancólico,
guitarrista lunático, poeta,
y pobre hombre en sueños,
siempre buscando a Dios entre la niebla.

LXXVIII

¿Y ha de morir contigo el mundo mago
donde guarda el recuerdo
los hálitos más puros de la vida,
la blanca sombra del amor primero,
    la voz que fue a tu corazón, la mano
que tú querías retener en sueños,
y todos los amores
que llegaron al alma, al hondo cielo?
    ¿Y ha de morir contigo el mundo tuyo,
la vieja vida en orden tuyo y nuevo?
¿Los yunques y crisoles de tu alma
trabajan para el polvo y para el viento?

Like an abandoned dog
without trail or scent,
straying down purposeless paths,
like a child on a festive night,
    lost among all the people
and the dust and the sparkling flares,
bewildered, his heart burdened
by the music and his distress—
    that's how I am: a melancholy drunk,
a moonstruck guitarist, a poet,
a wretch lost in dreams,
forever seeking God in the mist.

LXXVIII

And must it die with you, the magic world
where memories treasure
the purest breaths of life,
the white shadow of first love,
    the voice that reached your heart, the hand
you wished to go on holding in your dreams,
and all the loves
    that touched the soul, the deepest sky?
    And must it die with you, your very world,
the old life shaped in your new ways ?
    And are the anvils and crucibles of your soul
working just for the dust and the wind?

LXXXV

La primavera besaba
suavemente la arboleda,
y el verde nuevo brotaba
como una verde humareda.
   Las nubes iban pasando
sobre el campo juvenil . . .
Yo vi en las hojas temblando
las frescas lluvias de abril .
   Bajo ese almendro florído,
todo cargado de flor
—recordé—, yo he maldecido
mi juventud sin amor.
   Hoy, en mitad de la vida,
me he parado a meditar . . .
¡Juventud nunca vivida,
quién te volviera a soñar!

LXXXV

Spring gently
kissed the grove,
and fresh green sprang
like a green haze.
     Clouds were floating
over the youthful field . . .
Trembling in the leaves,
I saw fresh April showers.
     Under that almond blossom,
weighed down with its blooms—
I remembered—I cursed
my loveless youth.
     Today, in middle age,
I have paused to meditate . . .
Youth that I never lived,
would that I could dream you again!

LXXXVII
RENACIMIENTO

Galerías del alma . . . ¡El alma niña!
Su clara luz risueña;
y la pequeña historia ,
y la alegría de la vida nueva . . .
    ¡Ah, volver a nacer, y andar camino,
ya recobrada la perdida senda!
    Y volver a sentir en nuestra mano,
aquel latido de la mano buena
de nuestra madre . . . Y caminar en sueños
por amor de la mano que nos lleva.

*

En nuestras almas todo
por misteriosa mano se gobierna.
Incomprensibles, mudas,
nada sabemos de las almas nuestras.
    Las más hondas palabras
del sabio nos enseñan
lo que el silbar del viento cuando sopla
o el sonar de las aguas cuando ruedan.

LXXXVII
REBIRTH

Galleries of the soul . . . The young soul!
Its clear smiling light;
and its short story
and the joy of new life . . .
   Oh, to be born again, and to walk on ahead
after finding the lost path!
   And to feel in our hand, once again,
the pulse of the good hand
of our mother . . . And to walk in dreams
for love of the hand that guides us.

*

Everything in our souls
is governed by a mysterious hand.
We know nothing of our own souls,
incomprehensible, silent.
   The deepest words
of the wise man teach us
no more than the whistle of the wind as it blows
or the sound of the waters as they flow.

12. *"Between San Polo and San Saturio"*
(See Poem CXIII; *Around Soria* VIII, p.61)

Lands of Castile
(1907 - 1917)

Campos de Castilla

13. *top:* Mules drinking at a fountain in Soria, c. 1910.
14. *bottom:* La Audiencia. *"The courthouse clock strikes one..."*
(See Poem CXIII; *Around Soria* VI)

15. San Polo. See Poem CXIII; *Around Soria* VII

16. Romería on the banks of the Duero.

XCVII
RETRATO

Mi infancia son recuerdos de un patio de Sevilla,
y un huerto claro donde madura el limonero;
mi juventud, veinte años en tierra de Castilla;
mi historia, algunos casos que recordar no quiero.
Ni un seductor Mañara, ni un Bradomín he sido
—ya conocéis mi torpe aliño indumentario—,
mas recibí la flecha que me asignó Cupido,
y amé cuanto ellas puedan tener de hospitalario.
Hay en mis venas gotas de sangre jacobina,
pero mi verso brota de manantial sereno;
y, más que un hombre al uso que sabe su doctrina,
soy, en el buen sentido de la palabra, bueno.
Adoro la hermosura, y en la moderna estética
corté las viejas rosas del huerto de Ronsard;
mas no amo los afeites de la actual cosmética,
ni soy un ave de esas del nuevo gay-trinar.
Desdeño las romanzas de los tenores huecos
y el coro de los grillos que cantan a la luna.
A distinguir me paro las voces de los ecos,
y escucho solamente, entre las voces, una.
¿Soy clásico o romántico? No sé. Dejar quisiera
mi verso, como deja el capitán su espada:
famosa por la mano viril que la blandiera,
no por el docto oficio del forjador preciada.
Converso con el hombre que siempre va conmigo
—quien habla solo espera hablar a Dios un día—;

XCVII
PORTRAIT[6]

My childhood is memories of a courtyard in Seville
and a sunlit garden with ripening lemons;
my youth, twenty years in the lands of Castile;
my story, some events I would rather not tell.

In my dealings with women I've been no Don Juan
(I could never be bothered to dress for the part),
but I received the dart allotted me by Cupid
and have enjoyed all the comforts women bring.

Through my veins flow drops of rebel blood,
but my verse rises from a calm and clear spring;
and, more than the learned, fashionable pious,
I am, in the true meaning of the word, good.

I adore beauty, and in the modern fashion
I plucked the old roses from Ronsard's garden;
But I hate the excesses of modern cosmetics,
and I refuse to trill to the latest tune.

I disdain the ballads of hollow tenors
and the chorus of crickets singing to the moon.
I pause to distinguish voices from echoes
and among all the voices listen to but one.

Am I classical or romantic? Who knows? I wish
to bequeath my verse, as a captain leaves his sword,
famous for the virile hand that brandished it,
not valued for the forger's precious art.

I talk to the man who always walks with me—
solitaries hope to talk to God one day.

mi soliloquio es plática con este buen amigo
que me enseñó el secreto de la filantropía.
Y al cabo, nada os debo; debéisme cuanto he escrito.
A mi trabajo acudo, con mi dinero pago
el traje que me cubre y la mansión que habito,
el pan que me alimenta y el lecho en donde yago.
Y cuando llegue el día del último viaje,
y esté al partir la nave que nunca ha de tornar,
me encontraréis a bordo ligero de equipaje,
casi desnudo, como los hijos de la mar.

[1906]

XCVIII
A ORILLAS DEL DUERO

Mediaba el mes de julio. Era un hermoso día.
Yo, solo, por las quiebras del pedregal subía,
buscando los recodos de sombra, lentamente.
A trechos me paraba para enjugar mi frente
y dar algún respiro al pecho jadeante;
o bien, ahincando el paso, el cuerpo hacia adelante
y hacia la mano diestra vencido y apoyado
en un bastón, a guisa de pastoril cayado,
trepaba por los cerros que habitan las rapaces
aves de altura, hollando las hierbas montaraces
de fuerte olor —romero, tomillo, salvia, espliego—.
Sobre los agrios campos caía un sol de fuego.
    Un buitre de anchas alas con majestuoso vuelo
cruzaba solitario el puro azul del cielo.

My soliloquies are chats with this good friend
who taught me the secret of loving humankind.
    In the end, I owe you nothing; you owe me all I've
written.
I bend to my work, with my earnings I pay
for the clothes that cover me and the house I inhabit,
for the bread I live on and the bed in which I lie.
    And when the day for the last journey comes,
and the ship of no return is ready to set sail,
you will find me on board travelling light,
practically naked, like the children of the sea.

                                              [1906]

XCVIII
ON THE BANKS OF THE DUERO

It was mid-July and a beautiful day.
Alone, I climbed gullies in the rocky scree,
moving slowly, seeking folds of shade.
From time to time I paused to mop my brow
and find some respite for my heaving chest;
then hurried on, my body bending forward
and to my right, spent but supported
on my stick, like a shepherd on his crook.
So I climbed to the heights where great birds
of prey live, treading the strong-scented
highland herbs—rosemary, thyme, lavender and sage.
A fiery sun blazed down on the sour fields.
A broad-winged vulture, in majestic flight,
lone in the sky, crossed the clear blue.

Yo divisaba, lejos, un monte alto y agudo,
y una redonda loma cual recamado escudo,
y cárdenos alcores sobre la parda tierra
—harapos esparcidos de un viejo arnés de guerra—,
las serrezuelas calvas por donde tuerce el Duero
para formar la corva ballesta de un arquero
en torno a Soria. —Soria es una barbacana,
hacia Aragón, que tiene la torre castellana—.
Veía el horizonte cerrado por colinas
oscuras, coronadas de robles y de encinas;
desnudos peñascales, algún humilde prado
donde el merino pace y el toro, arrodillado
sobre la hierba, rumia; las márgenes del río
lucir sus verdes álamos al claro sol de estío,
y, silenciosamente, lejanos pasajeros,
¡tan diminutos! —carros, jinetes y arrieros—,
cruzar el largo puente, y bajo las arcadas
de piedra ensombrecerse las aguas plateadas
del Duero.
     El Duero cruza el corazón de roble
de Iberia y de Castilla.
                              ¡Oh, tierra triste y noble,
la de los altos llanos y yermos y roquedas,
de campos sin arados, regatos ni arboledas;
decrépitas ciudades, caminos sin mesones,
y atónitos palurdos sin danzas ni canciones
que aún van, abandonando el mortecino hogar,
como tus largos ríos, Castilla, hacia la mar!
     Castilla miserable, ayer dominadora,
envuelta en sus andrajos desprecia cuanto ignora.
¿Espera, duerme o sueña? ¿La sangre derramada
recuerda, cuando tuvo la fiebre de la espada?
Todo se mueve, fluye, discurre, corre o gira;
cambian la mar y el monte y el ojo que los mira.

I could see, far off, a sharp mountain peak
and a rounded shoulder, like an embroidered shield,
and purple mounds rising from tawny earth—
scattered remnants of an ancient suit of armour—
the barren ranges where the Duero twists
to draw its crossbow curve
round Soria. Soria is a barbican
pointing to Aragon, with its tower in Castile.
I saw the horizon enclosed by dark hills
crowned with holm oaks and scrub;
naked rocks, some humble meadows
where merinos grazed and a kneeling bull
ruminated on grass; river banks thrusting
green poplars into the summer sun;
and silently, some far-off travellers,
so small —carts, horsemen, muleteers—
crossed the long bridge, while under the stone
arches the Duero's silvered waters
darkened.
        The Duero crosses the oaken heart
of Iberia and Castile.
                Sad and noble land,
land of high plateaus, of wilderness and rock,
of fields unploughed, no watercourse or grove;
of crumbling cities, of roads without inns,
and bewildered rustics with no dance or song
who still flow, leaving their dying hearths,
like your long rivers, Castile, to the sea.
Wretched Castile, once the proud ruler,
wrapped in her rags, disdaining the unknown.
Does she sleep, wait, or dream? Does she recall
the blood spilt in fierce recourse to the sword?
Everything stirs, flows, wanders, turns or runs;
the seas change with the land and the observer's eyes.

¿Pasó? Sobre sus campos aún el fantasma yerra
de un pueblo que ponía a Dios sobre la guerra.
   La madre en otro tiempo fecunda en capitanes,
madrastra es hoy apenas de humildes ganapanes.
Castilla no es aquélla tan generosa un día,
cuando Myo Cid Rodrigo el de Viva volvía,
ufano de su nueva fortuna, y su opulencia,
a regalar a Alfonso los huertos de Valencia;
o que, tras la aventura que acreditó sus bríos,
pedía la conquista de los inmensos ríos
indianos a la corte, la madre de soldados,
guerreros y adalides que han de tornar, cargados
de plata y oro, a España, en regios galeones,
para la presa cuervos, para la lid leones.
Filósofos nutridos de sopa de convento
contemplan impasibles el amplio firmamento;
y si les llega en sueños, como un rumor distante,
clamor de mercaderes de muelles de Levante,
no acudirán siquiera a preguntar ¿qué pasa?
Y ya la guerra ha abierto las puertas de su casa.
   Castilla miserable, ayer dominadora,
envuelta en sus harapos desprecia cuanto ignora.
   El sol va declinando. De la ciudad lejana
me llega un armonioso tañido de campana
—ya irán a su rosario las enlutadas viejas—,
De entre las peñas salen dos lindas comadrejas;
me miran y se alejan, huyendo, y aparecen
de nuevo, ¡tan curiosas! . . . Los campos se oscurecen.
Hacia el camino blanco está el mesón abierto
al campo ensombrecido y al pedregal desierto.

Has she gone? Over her fields still roams the ghost
of a people who set their God above war.
The once fertile mother of so many brave captains,
now barely a stepmother to indigent louts.
Once-generous Castile, long gone is the day
when Rodrigo of Vivar[7]—El Cid—returned exulting
in his newly won fortune and wealth
to lay the groves of Valencia at the feet of Alfonso;
or when, after the deeds that proved your spirit,
you asked the court for the right to plunder
huge rivers of Indies; mother of soldiers,
warriors, champions, coming back laden
with silver and gold, to Spain, in proud galleons;
ravenous for their quarry, lions in the battle.
Now philosophers nurtured on convent scraps
listlessly gaze at the endless skies;
and if in their dreams they hear the far roar
of bustling merchants on the quays to the east,
they will not trouble even to ask what it is—
and now war has forced open the gates of your house.
Wretched Castile, former proud ruler,
shrouded in tatters, despising the unknown.
The sun is setting. A harmonious peal of bells
reaches my ears from the distant city—
time for the rosary for old women in black.
Two neat little weasels slip out from the rocks,
stare at me, flee, peer out once again—
so curious! The plain grows dark.
Over by the white road the inn door opens
on the sombre fields and the rock-strewn wastes.

CXIII
CAMPOS DE SORIA

I

Es la tierra de Soria árida y fría.
Por las colinas y las sierras calvas,
verdes pradillos, cerros cenicientos,
la primavera pasa
dejando entre las hierbas olorosas
sus diminutas margaritas blancas.
　　La tierra no revive, el campo sueña.
Al empezar abril está nevada
la espalda del Moncayo;
el caminante lleva en su bufanda
envueltos cuello y boca, y los pastores
pasan cubiertos con sus luengas capas.

II

Las tierras labrantías,
como retazos de estameñas pardas,
el huertecillo, el abejar, los trozos
de verde obscuro en que el merino pasta,
entre plomizos peñascales, siembran
el sueño alegre de infantil Arcadia.
En los chopos lejanos del camino,
parecen humear las yertas ramas
como un glauco vapor —las nuevas hojas—
y en las quiebras de valles y barrancas
blanquean los zarzales florecidos,
y brotan las violetas perfumadas.

CXIII
AROUND SORIA[8]

I

The land around Soria is arid and cold.
Spring moves over
the hills and bald uplands,
little green meadows, ashen crests,
leaving its tiny white daisies
scattered in the scented grasses.
The land is not reborn; the earth
is dreaming. In early April snow
clings to the Moncayo's brow;
travellers' necks and mouths
are wrapped in scarves, and shepherds
shelter in their ample cloaks.

II

The ploughed fields,
like snippets of dark serge,
the little orchards, beehives, strips
of dark green where merinos graze,
among leaden crags, sow
happy dreams of Arcadian childhood.
On the distant poplars by the road
the stiff branches seem to steam
in a glaucous haze—new leaves—
and in the fissures of valleys and gullies
brambles grow white with blooms
and scented violets burgeon.

III

Es el campo ondulado, y los caminos
ya ocultan los viajeros que cabalgan
en pardos borriquillos,
ya al fondo de la tarde arrebolada
elevan las plebeyas figurillas,
que el lienzo de oro del ocaso manchan.
Mas si trepáis a un cerro y veis el campo
desde los picos donde habita el águila,
son tornasoles de carmín y acero,
llanos plomizos, lomas plateadas,
circuidos por montes de violeta,
con las cumbres de nieve sonrosada.

IV

¡Las figuras del campo sobre el cielo!
Dos lentos bueyes aran
en un alcor, cuando el otoño empieza,
y entre las negras testas doblegadas
bajo el pesado yugo,
pende un cesto de juncos y retama,
que es la cuna de un niño;
y tras la yunta marcha
un hombre que se inclina hacia la tierra,
y una mujer que en las abiertas zanjas
arroja la semilla.
Bajo una nube de carmín y llama,
en el oro fluido y verdinoso
del poniente, las sombras se agigantan.

III

This is rolling land: the roads
at times hide travellers riding
little grey donkeys, then,
a backdrop on the reddened evening,
raise peasant silhouettes that spot
the gold cloth of the sunset sky.
But if you climb a hill and see the land
from the peaks where the eagles live,
there are sheens of carmine and steel,
ashen plains, silvered slopes,
surrounded by violet mountains,
their snowy summits shot with rose.

IV

The country shapes against the sky!
Two slow oxen ploughing
on a hillock in early autumn:
between their black heads bent
beneath the heavy yoke
hangs a basket of rushes and broom,
which is a cradle for a child;
and behind the team walk
a man bending toward the earth
and a woman casting seed
into the open furrows.
Beneath a flame and carmine cloud,
in the streaming, greenish gold
of sunset, shadows grow huge.

V

La nieve. En el mesón al campo abierto
se ve el hogar donde la leña humea
y la olla al hervir borbollonea.
El cierzo corre por el campo yerto,
alborotando en blancos torbellinos
la nieve silenciosa.
La nieve sobre el campo y los caminos
cayendo está como sobre una fosa.
Un viejo acurrucado tiembla y tose
cerca del fuego; su mechón de lana
la vieja hila, y una niña cose
verde ribete a su estameña grana.
Padres los viejos son de un arriero
que caminó sobre la blanca tierra
y una noche perdió ruta y sendero,
y se enterró en las nieves de la sierra.
En torno al fuego hay un lugar vacío,
y en la frente del viejo, de hosco ceño,
como un tachón sombrío
—tal el golpe de un hacha sobre un leño—.
La vieja mira al campo, cual si oyera
pasos sobre la nieve. Nadie pasa.
Desierta la vecina carretera,
desierto el campo en torno de la casa.
La niña piensa que en los verdes prados
ha de correr con otras doncellitas
en los días azules y dorados,
cuando crecen las blancas margaritas.

V

Snow. In the inn open to the fields
you can see the hearth with smoking logs
and the pot bubbling as it boils.
The north wind sweeps the frozen ground,
whipping up the silent snow
into white whirlwinds.
Snow is falling on fields and roads
as though into an open grave.
Huddled by the fire, an old man
shakes and coughs; the old woman
spins her woollen thread, and a girl sews
a green border on her scarlet serge.
The old people are the parents of a muleteer
who travelled over the white land
and one night lost his way and the path
and was buried in the snows of the sierra.
Around the fire there's an empty place
and on the old man's sombre brow
a sort of darkened furrow—
like the gash from an axe on a log.
The old woman looks out, as if hearing
footsteps in the snow. No one goes by.
The nearby road's deserted, as are
the fields around the house.
The girl is seeing herself running
with other maidens in green meadows
in the blue and golden days
when the white daisies flourish.

VI

¡Soria fría, *Soria pura*,
cabeza de Extremadura,
con su castillo guerrero
arruinado, sobre el Duero;
con sus murallas roídas
y sus casas denegridas!
    ¡Muerta ciudad de señores,
soldados o cazadores;
de portales con escudos
con cien linajes hidalgos,
y de famélicos galgos,
de galgos flacos y agudos,
que pululan
por las sórdidas callejas,
y a la medianoche ululan,
cuando graznan las cornejas!
    ¡Soria fría! La campana
de la Audiencia da la una.
Soria, cuidad castellana
¡tan bella! bajo la luna.

VII

¡Colinas plateadas,
grises alcores, cárdenas roquedas
por donde traza el Duero
su curva de ballesta
en torno a Soria, obscuros encinares,
ariscos pedregales, calvas sierras,
caminos blancos y álamos del río,
tardes de Soria, mística y guerrera,
hoy siento por vosotros, en el fondo
del corazón, tristeza,
tristeza que es amor! ¡Campos de Soria
donde parece que las rocas sueñan,
conmigo vais! ¡Colinas plateadas,
grises alcores, cárdenas roquedas! . . .

VI

Cold Soria! *Pure Soria,*
head of Extremadura,[9]
with its warrior castle
in ruins above the Duero,
with its crumbling walls
and its blackened houses!
   Dead city of proud
soldiers or hunters,
of doorways emblazoned
with a hundred lineages,
and of starving greyhounds,
greyhounds thin and sharp,
who swarm
through the filthy alleys
and howl at midnight
when the crows caw!
   Cold Soria! The courthouse
clock strikes one.
Soria, Castilian city,
so beautiful beneath the moon!

VII

Silvered slopes,
grey hillocks, purple rocks
through which the Duero draws
its crossbow curve
round Soria, dark oak groves,
wild screes, bald mountain-tops,
white roads and river poplars,
evenings of Soria, mystic and warrior,
today I feel for you, in the depths
of my heart, sorrow,
sorrow that is love! Lands of Soria
where the rocks seem to dream—
you go with me! Silvered slopes,
grey hillocks, purple rocks!

VIII

He vuelto a ver los álamos dorados,
álamos del camino en la ribera
del Duero, entre San Polo y San Saturio,
tras las murallas viejas
de Soria —barbacana
hacia Aragón, en castellana tierra—.
Estos chopos del río, que acompañan
con el sonido de sus hojas secas
el son del agua, cuando el viento sopla,
tienen en sus cortezas
grabadas iniciales que son nombres
de enamorados, cifras que son fechas.
¡Álamos del amor que ayer tuvisteis
de ruiseñores vuestras ramas llenas;
álamos que seréis mañana liras
del viento perfumado en primavera;
álamos del amor cerca del agua
que corre y pasa y sueña,
álamos de las márgenes del Duero,
conmigo vais, mi corazón os lleva!

IX

¡Oh, sí! Conmigo vais, campos de Soria,
tardes tranquilas, montes de violeta,
alamedas del río, verde sueño
del suelo gris y de la parda tierra,
agria melancolía
de la ciudad decrépita.
Me habéis llegado al alma,
¿o acaso estabais en el fondo de ella?
¡Gentes del alto llano numantino
que a Dios guardáis como cristianas viejas,
que el sol de España os llene
de alegría, de luz y de riqueza!

VIII

Once more I've seen the golden poplars,
poplars along the path on the bank
of the Duero, between San Polo and San Saturio,[10]
behind the old walls
of Soria—a barbican
facing Aragon, on the soil of Castile.
   These poplars by the river,
whose dry leaves rustle
to the water's tune when the wind blows,
have initials carved
on their bark—the names of lovers,
with numbers telling dates.
Poplars of love, whose branches yesterday
were filled with nightingales;
poplars that tomorrow will be lyres
for the scented breeze of spring;
poplars of love down by the water,
which runs and flows and dreams;
poplars of the Duero river banks,
you go with me: I bear you in my heart!

IX

Oh, yes! You go with me, you lands of Soria,
tranquil evenings, violet mountains,
river-lining poplars, green dream
of the grey ground and the drab land,
bitter melancholy
of the crumbling city.
You have reached into my soul—
or were you already in its depths?
People of the high Numantian plain,[11]
who guard God like old Christians,
may the sun of Spain fill you
with joy, with light and wealth!

CXV
A UN OLMO SECO

Al olmo viejo, hendido por el rayo
y en su mitad podrido,
con las lluvias de abril y el sol de mayo,
algunas hojas verdes le han salido.
    ¡El olmo centenario en la colina
que lame el Duero! Un musgo amarillento
le mancha la corteza blanquecina
al tronco carcomido y polvoriento.
    No será, cual los álamos cantores
que guardan el camino y la ribera,
habitado de pardos ruiseñores.
    Ejército de hormigas en hilera
va trepando por él, y en sus entrañas
urden sus telas grises las arañas.
    Antes que te derribe, olmo del Duero,
con su hacha el leñador, y el carpintero
te convierta en melena de campana,
lanza de carro o yugo de carreta;
antes que rojo en el hogar, mañana,
ardas de alguna mísera caseta,
al borde de un camino;
antes que te descuaje un torbellino
y tronche el soplo de las sierras blancas;
antes que el río hasta la mar te empuje
por valles y barrancas,
olmo, quiero anotar en mi cartera
la gracia de tu rama verdecida.
Mi corazón espera
también, hacia la luz y hacia la vida,
otro milagro de la primavera.

Soria, 1912

CXV
TO A WITHERED ELM[12]

The old elm, split by lightning
and now rotten to the heart,
with April rains and May sun
has produced a few green leaves.
    Oh ageless elm on the hill
the Duero licks! A sallow moss
stains the whitish bark
of its worm-eaten, dusty trunk.
    Unlike the singing poplars
that guard the track and bank
it will house no dun nightingales.
    An army of ants in single file
winds up and down, while spiders
weave their grey webs in its guts.
    Before the woodman's axe fells you,
Duero elm, and the carpenter
makes you into bell stays,
cart shafts, or oxen yokes;
before you burn tomorrow,
glowing in some poor
roadside cottage hearth;
before a whirlwind uproots you
or the white peaks' blast breaks you;
before the river bears you seaward
through valleys and ravines,
old elm, I want to note and record
the grace of your green shoot.
    My heart too hopes,
trusting in light and life,
for another miracle from spring.

Soria, 1912

CXVII
AL MAESTRO "AZORÍN" POR SU LIBRO *CASTILLA*

La venta de Cidones está en la carretera
que va de Soria a Burgos. Leonarda, la ventera,
que llaman la Ruipérez, es una viejecita
que aviva el fuego donde borbolla la marmita.
Ruipérez, el ventero, un viejo diminuto
—bajo las cejas grises, dos ojos de hombre astuto—,
contempla silencioso la lumbre del hogar.
Se oye la marmita al fuego borbollar.
Sentado ante una mesa de pino, un caballero
escribe. Cuando moja la pluma en el tintero,
dos ojos tristes lucen en un semblante enjuto.
El caballero es joven, vestido va de luto.
El viento frío azota los chopos del camino.
Se ve pasar de polvo un blanco remolino.
La tarde se va haciendo sombría. El enlutado,
la mano en la mejilla, medita ensimismado.
Cuando el correo llegue, que el caballero aguarda,
la tarde habrá caído sobre la tierra parda
de Soria. Todavía los grises serrijones,
con ruinas de encinares y mellas de aluviones,
las lomas azuladas, las agrias barranqueras,
picotas y colinas, ribazos y laderas
del páramo sombrío por donde cruza el Duero,
darán al sol de ocaso su resplandor de acero.
La venta se oscurece. El rojo lar humea.
La mecha de un mohoso candil arde y chispea.
El enlutado tiene clavados en el fuego
los ojos largo rato; se los enjuga luego
con un pañuelo blanco. ¿Por qué le hará llorar
el son de la marmita, el ascua del hogar?
Cerró la noche. Lejos se escucha el traqueteo
y el galopar de un coche que avanza. Es el correo.

CXVII
TO THE MASTER, "AZORIN" FOR HIS BOOK *CASTILLA*[13]

Cidones Inn stands on the main road
from Soria to Burgos. The landlady, Leonarda—
or just "Ruipérez's wife"— is a little old lady
kindling the fire on which the iron pot boils.
Ruipérez, the landlord, a shrivelled old man
with two shrewd eyes under grey brows,
silently watches the flames in the hearth.
You can hear the pot boiling on the fire.
Seated at a pine table, a gentleman
is writing. When he dips his pen in the inkwell,
two sad eyes gleam in a lean face.
The gentleman is young and dressed in mourning.
The cold wind whips the poplars by the roadside.
An eddy of white dust whirls past.
The evening grows darker. The mourner,
hand on cheek, sits rapt in thought.
By the time the mail coach he awaits arrives
dusk will have fallen over the drab land
of Soria. By then the grey crags
with ruined oaks and stone-strewn gaps,
the bluish ridges, harsh ravines,
heights and hillsides, banks and slopes
of the sombre plateau the Duero crosses
will show the setting sun their steely sheen.
The inn grows dark. The red hearth smokes.
The wick of a rusty oil-lamp burns and splutters.
The mourner fixes his gaze a good while
on the fire; then dries his eyes
with a white handkerchief. Why should the sound
of the pot, the burning embers, make him weep?
Night has closed in. Far off, a clatter of wheels
and thud of hooves from an approaching coach.
    It's the mail.

CXIX

Señor, ya me arrancaste lo que yo más quería.
Oye otra vez, Dios mío, mi corazón clamar.
Tu voluntad se hizo, Señor, contra la mía.
Señor, ya estamos solos mi corazón y el mar.

CXXI

Allá, en las tierras altas,
por donde traza el Duero
su curva de ballesta
en torno a Soria, entre plomizos cerros
y manchas de raídos encinares,
mi corazón está vagando, en sueños . . .
    ¿No ves, Leonor, los álamos del río
con sus ramajes yertos?
Mira el Moncayo azul y blanco; dame
tu mano y paseemos.
Por estos campos de la tierra mía,
bordados de olivares polvorientos,
voy caminando solo,
triste, cansado, pensativo y viejo.

CXIX

Lord, you have torn from me what I loved most.
Once more, my God, hear my heart plead.
Thy will, not mine, O Lord, was done.
Now, Lord, we're alone—my heart and the sea.

CXXI

Up there, on the high plateau,
where the Duero draws
its crossbow curve
round Soria, through leaden hills
and patches of frayed ilex,
my heart is wandering in dreams. . . .
 Can't you see, Leonor, the poplars by the river
with their stiff branches?
Look at the Moncayo, blue and white;
give me your hand, and let's walk.
Through these fields of my homeland,
embroidered with dusty olive groves,
I go walking alone,
sad, tired, brooding and old.

CXXII

Soñé que tú me llevabas
por una blanca vereda,
en medio del campo verde,
hacia el azul de las sierras,
hacia los montes azules,
una mañana serena.
   Sentí tu mano en la mía,
tu mano de compañera,
tu voz de niña en mi oído
como una campana nueva,
como una campana virgen
de un alba de primavera.
¡Eran tu voz y tu mano,
en sueños, tan verdaderas! . . .
Vive, esperanza, ¡quién sabe
lo que se traga la tierra!

CXXIII

Una noche de verano
—estaba abierto el balcón
y la puerta de mi casa—
la muerte en mi casa entró.
Se fue acercando a su lecho
—ni siquiera me miró—,
con unos dedos muy finos
algo muy tenue rompió.
Silenciosa y sin mirarme,
la muerte otra vez pasó
delante de mí. ¿Qué has hecho?
La muerte no respondió.
Mi niña quedó tranquila,
dolido mi corazón.
¡Ay, que lo que la muerte ha roto
era un hilo entre los dos!

CXXII

I dreamt you were leading me
along a white path,
across green fields
toward the blue peaks,
toward the blue mountains,
one peaceful morning.
 I felt your hand in mine,
your true friend's hand,
your girlish voice in my ear
like the sound of a new bell,
like a virgin bell ringing
at the break of a spring dawn.
Your voice and your hand
were so real—in my dreams.
Hope, live on! Who knows
what earth absorbs?

CXXIII

One summer night—
my balcony was open
and the door of my house—
death entered my house.
It approached her bed,
not even looking at me,
and with such thin fingers
snapped something so fine.
Silent, not looking at me,
death passed once more
before me. What have you done ?
Death gave no answer.
My girl was peaceful;
my heart was in pain.
What death has snapped
was a thread between us two!

CXXVI
A JOSÉ MARÍA PALACIO

Palacio, buen amigo,
¿está la primavera
vistiendo ya las ramas de los chopos
del río y los caminos? En la estepa
del alto Duero, primavera tarda,
¡pero es tan bella y dulce cuando llega! . . .
¿Tienen los viejos olmos
algunas hojas nuevas?
Aún las acacias estarán desnudas
y nevados los montes de las sierras.
¡Oh mole del Moncayo blanca y rosa,
allá, en el cielo de Aragón, tan bella!
¿Hay zarzas florecidas
entre las grises peñas,
y blancas margaritas
entre la fina hierba?
Por esos campanarios
ya habrán ido llegando las cigüeñas.
Habrá trigales verdes,
y mulas pardas en las sementeras,
y labriegos que siembran los tardíos
con las lluvias de abril. Ya las abejas
libarán del tomillo y el romero.
¿Hay ciruelos en flor? ¿Quedan violetas?
Furtivos cazadores, los reclamos
de la perdiz bajo las capas luengas,
no faltarán. Palacio, buen amigo,
¿tienen ya ruiseñores las riberas?
Con los primeros lirios
y las primeras rosas de las huertas,
en una tarde azul, sube al Espino.
al alto Espino donde está su tierra . . .

Baeza, 29 de abril de 1913

CXXVI
TO JOSÉ MARÍA PALACIO[14]

Palacio, good friend,
is spring now decking
the branches of the poplars
by the river and the roads? On the steppes
of the upper Duero, spring holds back,
but it's so beautiful and sweet when it arrives!
Do the old elm trees
have any new leaves?
The acacias will still be bare—
snow on the slopes of the mountains.
Oh, the mass of the Moncayo, white and pink,
in the distant Aragon skies, so fine!
Are there brambles flowering
among the grey rocks
and white marguerites
in the delicate grass?
By now, the storks will be nesting
on all the bell towers.
There will be green wheat
and dusky mules in the fields
and peasants sowing their late crops
under April showers. By now the bees
can sip thyme and rosemary.
Are the plum trees in blossom? Violets still out?
Poachers hiding decoy
partridges under long cloaks
will surely be there. Palacio, good friend,
are there still nightingales on the banks?
With the first lilies
and early roses from the gardens,
on a blue afternoon, go up to the Espino,
to the high Espino where her ground is.

Baeza, 29 April 1913

CXXIX
NOVIEMBRE 1913

Un año más. El sembrador va echando
la semilla en los surcos de la tierra.
Dos lentas yuntas aran,
mientras pasan las nubes cenicientas
ensombreciendo el campo,
las pardas sementeras,
los grises olivares. Por el fondo
del valle el río el agua turbia lleva.
Tiene Cazorla nieve,
y Mágina, tormenta,
su montera, Aznaitín. Hacia Granada,
montes con sol, montes de sol y piedra.

CXXIX
NOVEMBER 1913[15]

Another year gone. The sower casts
the seed in the furrows of the earth.
Two slow yokes of oxen plough
while ashen clouds blow past,
shadowing the land,
the dun sown fields,
grey olive groves. At the bottom
of the valley the river flows muddy.
There's snow on Cazorla,
a storm over Mágina,
cloud cap on Aznaitín. By Granada,
sun on the mountains, mountains of sun and stone.

CXXX
LA SAETA

¿Quién me presta una escalera
para subir al madero,
para quitarle los clavos
a Jesús el Nazareno?

Saeta Popular

¡Oh, la saeta, el cantar
al Cristo de los gitanos,
siempre con sangre en las manos,
siempre por desenclavar!
¡Cantar del pueblo andaluz,
que todas las primaveras
anda pidiendo escaleras
para subir a la cruz!
¡Cantar de la tierra mía,
que echa flores
al Jesús de la agonía,
y es la fe de mis mayores!
¡Oh, no eres tú mi cantar!
¡No puedo cantar, ni quiero
a ese Jesús del madero,
sino al que anduvo en el mar!

CXXX
THE *SAETA*[16]

Who will lend me a ladder
to climb the tree
and pull out the nails
from Jesus the Nazarene?
(Popular *saeta*)

Oh, the *saeta*, the song
to the Christ of the gypsies,
always with bleeding hands,
always nailed to the cross!
The chant of Andalusia,
where every spring
they ask for ladders
to climb that tree!
Song of my homeland,
where they toss flowers
to Jesus in agony,
the faith of my elders!
Oh, you are not my song!
I cannot and will not sing
to this Jesus nailed to wood,
but to the one who walked on the sea.

CXXXI
DEL PASADO EFÍMERO

Este hombre del casino provinciano
que vio a Carancha recibir un día,
tiene mustia la tez, el pelo cano,
ojos velados por melancolía;
bajo el bigote gris, labios de hastío,
y una triste expresión, que no es tristeza,
sino algo más y menos: el vacío
del mundo en la oquedad de su cabeza.
Aún luce de corinto terciopelo
chaqueta y pantalón abotinado,
y un cordobés color de caramelo,
pulido y torneado.
Tres veces heredó; tres ha perdido
al monte su caudal; dos ha enviudado.
Sólo se anima ante el azar prohibido,
sobre el verde tapete reclinado,
o al evocar la tarde de un torero,
la suerte de un tahúr, o si alguien cuenta
la hazaña de un gallardo bandolero,
o la proeza de un matón, sangrienta.
Bosteza de política banales
dicterios al gobierno reaccionario,
y augura que vendrán los liberales,
cual torna la cigüeña al campanario.
Un poco labrador, del cielo aguarda
y al cielo teme; alguna vez suspira,
pensando en su olivar, y al cielo mira
con ojo inquieto, si la lluvia tarda.
Lo demás, taciturno, hipocondriaco,
prisionero en la Arcadia del presente,
le aburre; sólo el humo del tabaco
simula algunas sombras en su frente.

CXXXI
THE EPHEMERAL PAST[17]

This man in a provincial casino,
who once saw Carancha "receive",
has slack skin, grey hair,
eyes hooded with melancholy;
lips of boredom under his grizzled moustache,
and a sad expression that is not grief
but something more, and less—the void
of emptiness within his head.
He still sports a purplish velvet
jacket, laced-cuff trousers,
and a caramel *cordobés*,
well smoothed and brushed.
He was left money three times; three times
lost it at cards; twice been widowed.
He wakes up only for forbidden gaming,
leaning over the green baize,
or to evoke a bullfighter's brief glory,
a cardsharper's luck, or if someone tells
the deeds of a swashbuckling bandit
or the bloody prowess of some bully.
He yawns banal political
saws to the conservatives in power
and forecasts that the liberals will come
as storks return to their bell tower.
A bit of a peasant, he waits on the skies
and yet fears them; at times he sighs,
thinking of his olive grove, and looks
skyward anxiously, if the rains are late.
For the rest—taciturn, hypochondriac,
prisoner of passing pleasures—
he's bored; only tobacco smoke
casts false shadows on his brow.

Este hombre no es de ayer ni es de mañana,
sino de nunca; de la cepa hispana
no es el fruto maduro ni podrido,
es una fruta vana
de aquella España que pasó y no ha sido,
ésa que hoy tiene la cabeza cana.

CXXXV
EL MAÑANA EFÍMERO

A Roberto Castrovido.

La España de charanga y pandereta,
cerrado y sacristía,
devota de Frascuelo y de María,
de espíritu burlón y de alma inquieta,
ha de tener su mármol y su día,
su infalible mañana y su poeta.
El vano ayer engendrará un mañana
vacío y ¡por ventura! pasajero.
Será un joven lechuzo y tarambana,
un sayón con hechuras de bolero,
a la moda de Francia realista,
un poco al uso de París pagano,
y al estilo de España especialista
en el vicio al alcance de la mano.
Esa España inferior que ora y bosteza,
vieja y tahúr, zaragatera y triste;
esa España inferior que ora y embiste,
cuando se digna usar de la cabeza,
aún tendrá luengo parto de varones
amantes de sagradas tradiciones
y de sagradas formas y maneras;
florecerán las barbas apostólicas,
y otras calvas en otras calaveras
brillarán, venerables y católicas.

This man is not of yesterday nor of tomorrow
but of never: he is neither ripe nor rotten
fruit of Hispanic stock,
but an empty husk
of the Spain that passed and never was,
the one whose hair today is grey.

CXXXV
THE EPHEMERAL FUTURE[18]
For Roberto Castrovido

The Spain of brass bands and tambourines,
bull pens and sacristies,
devoted to Frascuelo and the Virgin,
with mocking heart and timid soul,
will get its marble tomb and end,
its infallible tomorrow and its poet.
The hollow past will spawn an empty
and—with luck!—transient future.
It will be a lazy, good-for-nothing youth,
a bolero-sporting bully,
in the style of royalist France,
something like pagan Paris,
but with a Spanish penchant
for the vice closest to hand.
This lower Spain that prays and yawns,
an ageing chancer, quarrelsome and sad;
this lower Spain that prays and charges,
when it deigns to use its head,
will still bring forth a progeny of youths
who love all that is traditional and sacred
and hallowed forms and manners;
more apostolic beards will grow,
and more bald pates on other skulls
will gleam, venerable and Catholic.

El vano ayer engendrará un mañana
vacío y ¡por ventura! pasajero,
la sombra de un lechuzo tarambana,
᾿de un sayón con hechuras de bolero;
el vacuo ayer dará un mañana huero.
Como la náusea de un borracho ahíto
de vino malo, un rojo sol corona
de heces turbias las cumbres de granito;
hay un mañana estomagante escrito
en la tarde pragmática y dulzona.
Mas otra España nace,
la España del cincel y de la maza,
con esa eterna juventud que se hace
del pasado macizo de la raza.
Una España implacable y redentora,
España que alborea
con un hacha en la mano vengadora,
España de la rabia y de la idea.

The hollow past will spawn an empty
and—with luck!—transient future,
the shadow of a lazy good-for-nothing,
of a bolero-sporting bully;
the vacuous past will give a sterile future.
Like the vomit of a drunkard gorged
on rotten wine, a red sun crowns
the granite peaks with sediment;
there's a sickening future written
in the cloying pragmatic evening.
But a different Spain is being born,
the Spain of chisel and mallet,
with the lasting youth that comes
from the solid past of the race.
An implacable, redeeming Spain,
a Spain that is dawning
with an axe in her avenging hand,
a Spain of ardour and ideas.

CXXXVII
PARÁBOLAS

I

Era un niño que soñaba
un caballo de cartón.
Abrió los ojos el niño
y el caballito no vio.
Con un caballito blanco
el niño volvió a soñar;
y por la crin lo cogía . . .
¡Ahora no te escaparás!
Apenas lo hubo cogido,
el niño se despertó.
Tenía el puño cerrado.
¡El caballito voló!
Quedóse el niño muy serio
pensando que no es verdad
un caballito soñado.
Y ya no volvió a soñar.
Pero el niño se hizo mozo
y el mozo tuvo un amor,
y a su amada le decía:
¿Tú eres de verdad o no?
Cuando el mozo se hizo viejo
pensaba: Todo es soñar,
el caballito soñado
y el caballo de verdad.
Y cuando vino la muerte,
el viejo a su corazón
preguntaba: ¿Tú eres sueño?
¡Quién sabe si despertó!

CXXXVII
PARABLES

I

There was a child who dreamt
of a cardboard horse.
The child opened his eyes
and couldn't see the horse.
The child dreamt again
of a little white horse;
he caught it by the mane . . .
"Now you won't get away!"
Just as he had caught it,
the child woke up.
His fist was closed,
but the horse had flown.
This left the child
seriously thinking
little dream horses aren't real.
And he never dreamed again.
But the child became a young man
and the young man fell in love
and asked his beloved,
"Are you real or not?"
When the young man was old
he thought: It's all a dream—
the little horse dreamed
and the real horse out there.
And when death came for him,
the old man asked his heart,
"Are you a dream?"
Who knows if he woke up!

CXXXIX
A DON FRANCISCO GINER DE LOS RÍOS

Como se fue el maestro,
la luz de esta mañana
me dijo: Van tres días
que mi hermano Francisco no trabaja.
¿Murió? ... Sólo sabemos
que se nos fue por una senda clara,
diciéndonos: Hacedme
un duelo de labores y esperanzas.
Sed buenos y no más, sed lo que he sido
entre vosotros: alma.
Vivid, la vida sigue,
los muertos mueren y las sombras pasan;
lleva quien deja y vive el que ha vivido.
¡Yunques, sonad; enmudeced, campanas!

    Y hacia otra luz más pura
partió el hermano de la luz del alba,
del sol de los talleres,
el viejo alegre de la vida santa.
... ¡Oh, sí!, llevad, amigos,
su cuerpo a la montaña,
a los azules montes
del ancho Guadarrama.
Allí hay barrancos hondos
de pinos verdes donde el viento canta.
Su corazón repose
bajo una encina casta,
en tierra de tomillos, donde juegan
mariposas doradas ...
Allí el maestro un día
soñaba un nuevo florecer de España.

Baeza, 21 de febrero de 1915

CXXXIX
FOR DON FRANCISCO GINER DE LOS RÍOS[19]

As the master went away,
this morning's light
told me: It is three days now
since my brother Francisco worked.
Did he die? . . . We only know
that he went from us down a bright path,
saying: Mourn me
in work and hope.
Be good and no more. Be what I
have been among you: spirit.
Live, for life goes on,
the dead die, and shadows pass;
those who have sown reap; those who lived still live.
Let anvils ring and bells be silent!
　　And the brother of the dawn light,
of the workshops filled with sun,
the happy old man of saintly life,
left us for a purer light.
　　Oh, yes!, friends, bear
his body to the mountains,
to the blue hills
of the broad Guadarrama,
with its deep ravines
of green pines where the wind sings.
Let his heart rest
beneath a pure ilex,
where wild thyme grows, where
golden butterflies play . . .
There one day the master
dreamt of Spain's rebirth.

Baeza, 21 February 1915

17. *"The old elm, split by lightning and now rotten to the heart."*
(See Poem CXV *To a Withered Elm*, p. 65)

New Songs
and later works

(1917–1930)

Nuevas Canciones
y obras posteriores

18. Street scene in Soria, c. 1900, showing El Círculo de la Amistad. *"This man in a provincial casino..."*
(See Poem CXXXI *The Ephemeral Past*, p. 79)

19. *"Cidones Inn stands on the main road."*
(See Poem CXVII *To the Master Azorín*, p. 67)

CLXI
PROVERBIOS Y CANTARES

A José Ortega y Gasset

I

El ojo que ves no es
ojo porque tú lo veas;
es ojo porque te ve.

IV

Mas busca en tu espejo al otro,
al otro que va contigo.

VIII

Hoy es siempre todavía.

XVI

Si vino la primavera,
volad a las flores;
no chupéis cera.

XVII

En mi soledad
he visto cosas muy claras,
que no son verdad.

LIII

Tras el vivir y el soñar,
está lo que más importa:
despertar.

CLXI
PROVERBS AND SONGS

For José Ortega y Gasset

I

The eye you see is not an eye
because you see it;
it is an eye for seeing you.

IV

Look in your mirror for the other,
the other who walks with you.

VIII

Today is still time.

XVI

If spring has come,
fly to the flowers:
don't suck wax.

XVII

In my solitude
I have very clearly seen
things that are not true.

LIII

After living and dreaming
comes what matters most:
waking up.

LXVI

Poned atención:
un corazón solitario
no es un corazón.

LXXXVII

¡Oh Guadalquivir!
Te vi en Cazorla nacer;
hoy, en Sanlúcar morir.
Un borbollón de agua clara,
debajo de un pino verde,
eras tú, ¡qué bien sonabas!
Como yo, cerca del mar,
río de barro salobre,
¿sueñas con tu manantial?

CLXV
IV

Esta luz de Sevilla . . . Es el palacio
donde nací, con su rumor de fuente.
Mi padre, en su despacho. —La alta frente,
la breve mosca, y el bigote lacio—.
Mi padre, aún joven. Lee, escribe, hojea
sus libros y medita. Se levanta;
va hacia la puerta del jardín. Pasea.
A veces habla solo, a veces canta.
Sus grandes ojos de mirar inquieto
ahora vagar parecen, sin objeto
donde puedan posar, en el vacío.
Ya escapan de su ayer a su mañana;
ya miran en el tiempo, ¡padre mío!,
piadosamente mi cabeza cana.

LXVI

Mark my words:
a lonely heart
is not a heart.

LXXXVII

Oh, Guadalquivir!
I saw you born in Cazorla;
today, dying in Sanlúcar.[20]
     You were a gush of clear water
beneath a green pine:
how sweet you sounded!
     Like me, by the sea,
river of brackish mud,
do you dream of your spring?

CLXV
IV[21]

This Seville light . . . is the mansion
I was born in, with its singing fountain.
My father in his study—lofty brow,
goatee beard, drooping moustache.
     My father, still young, reads, writes, leafs
through his books, ponders; he gets up,
goes towards the garden gate, and wanders.
Sometimes he talks to himself or sings.
     His large eyes with their restless look
now seem to drift in a void,
alighting on nothing fixed.
     Freed now from his past, they rove through time
to his tomorrow and come to rest—
dear father!—kindly on my grey head.

CLXIX
ÚLTIMAS LAMENTACIONES DE ABEL MARTÍN
(CANCIONERO APÓCRIFO)

Hoy, con la primavera,
soñé que un fino cuerpo me seguía
cual dócil sombra. Era
mi cuerpo juvenil, el que subía
le tres en tres peldaños la escalera.
     —Hola, galgo de ayer. (Su luz de acuario
trocaba el hondo espejo
por agria luz sobre un rincón de osario.)
     —¿Tú conmigo, rapaz?
     —Contigo, viejo.
Soñé la galería
al huerto de ciprés y limonero;
tibias palomas en la piedra fría,
en el cielo de añil rojo pandero,
y en la mágica angustia de la infancia
la vigilia del ángel más austero.
     La ausencia y la distancia
volví a soñar con túnicas de aurora;
firme en el arco tenso la saeta
del mañana, la vista aterradora
de la llama prendida en la espoleta
de su granada.
                    ¡Oh Tiempo, oh Todavía
preñado de inminencias!,
tú me acompañas en la senda fría,
tejedor de esperanzas e impaciencias.

                    *

     ¡El tiempo y sus banderas desplegadas!
(¿Yo, capitán? Mas yo no voy contigo.)
¡Hacia lejanas torres soleadas
el perdurable asalto por castigo!

CLXIX
LAST LAMENTS OF ABEL MARTÍN
(APOCRYPHAL SONGBOOK)

Today, as spring came,
I dreamt a slight figure was following me
like a meek shadow. It was
my boyhood body, the one that climbed
the stairs three steps at a time.
    "Greetings, former greyhound!" (Its aquarium light
bartered the depths of the mirror
for sharp light slanting on a bone yard.)
    "Are you with me, boy?"
                    "With you, old man."
I dreamt of the gallery leading
to the garden of cypress and lemon trees;
warm doves on cold stone,
a red kite high in the indigo sky,
and the sternest angel keeping watch
over childhood's magic anguish.
    Absence and distance
returned to my dreams robed in dawn;
tomorrow's arrow tense in the bow,
the terrifying sight
of the flame caught in the fuse
of its grenade.
          Oh, Time, oh Time
still pregnant with immediacy,
you will walk with me down the cold path,
weaver of hopes and frustrations!

*

Time and its unfurled flags!
("Me, captain? But I'm not going with you.")
The drawn-out punishment assault
on distant sunlit towers!

*

Hoy, como un día, en la ancha mar violeta
hunde el sueño su pétrea escalinata,
y hace camino la infantil goleta,
y le salta el delfín de bronce y plata.
    La hazaña y la aventura
cercando un corazón entelerido . . .
Montes de piedra dura
—eco y eco— mi voz han repetido.
    ¡Oh, descansar en el azul del día
como descansa el águila en el viento,
sobre la sierra fría,
segura de sus alas y su aliento!
    La augusta confianza
a ti, Naturaleza, y paz te pido,
mi tregua de temor y de esperanza,
un grano de alegría, un mar de olvido . . .

Today, as long ago, dreams sink
their stony steps in the broad, violet sea,
and the childish schooner sails on
with a bronze and silver dolphin leaping.
    Deeds and adventure enclosing
a heart shaking with fright. . . .
Hard stone hills—
echo on echo—have repeated my voice.
    Oh, to repose in the blue of the day
as an eagle rests on the wind
above the cold mountains,
sure of its breath and its wings!
    From you, Nature, I ask
lofty trust and peace,
my truce from fear and hope,
a grain of joy, an ocean of oblivion. . . .

CLXX
SIESTA

EN MEMORIA DE ABEL MARTÍN

Mientras traza su curva el pez de fuego,
junto al ciprés, bajo el supremo añil,
y vuela en blanca piedra el niño ciego,
y en el olmo la copla de marfil
de la verde cigarra late y suena,
honremos al Señor
—la negra estampa de su mano buena—
que ha dictado el silencio en el clamor.
　Al dios de la distancia y de la ausencia,
del áncora en el mar, la plena mar...
Él nos libra del mundo —omnipresencia—,
nos abre senda para caminar.
　Con la copa de sombra bien colmada,
con este nunca lleno corazón,
honremos al Señor que hizo la Nada
y ha esculpido en la fe nuestra razón.

CLXXIV

II

Todo amor es fantasía;
él inventa el año, el día,
la hora y su melodía;
inventa el amante y, más,
la amada. No prueba nada,
contra el amor, que la amada
no haya existido jamás.

CLXX
SIESTA

IN MEMORY OF ABEL MARTÍN

While the flaming fish draws its curve
by the cypress, under the indigo vault,
and the blind child flies in white stone,
and the ivory song of the green cicada
beats and resounds in the elm tree,
let us praise the Lord—
the black stamp of his good hand—
who has imposed silence on the clamour.
   The god of distance and of absence,
of the anchor in the sea, the high sea. . . .
He frees us from the world—omnipresence—
and opens up a path for us to walk.
   With our cup well filled with shadow,
with our hearts that are never filled,
let us praise the Lord who made Nothingness
and has sculpted our reason into faith.

CLXXIV

II

All love is fantasy;
it invents the year, the day,
the time and its tune;
it invents the lover and, still more,
the beloved. It is no proof
against love that the beloved
may never have existed.

CLXXV
MUERTE DE ABEL MARTÍN

Pensando que no veía
porque Dios no le miraba,
dijo Abel cuando moría:
Se acabó lo que se daba.

—J. De Mairena: *Epigramas*

I

Los últimos vencejos revolean
en torno al campanario;
los niños gritan, saltan, se pelean.
En su rincón, Martín el solitario.
¡La tarde, casi noche, polvorienta,
la algazara infantil, y el vocerío,
a la par de sus doce en sus cincuenta!

*

¡Oh alma plena y espíritu vacío,
ante la turbia hoguera
con llama restallante de raíces,
fogata de frontera
que ilumina las hondas cicatrices!

*

Quien se vive se pierde, Abel decía.
¡Oh distancia, distancia!, que la estrella
que nadie toca, guía.
¿Quién navegó sin ella?
Distancia para el ojo —¡oh lueñe nave!—,
ausencia al corazón empedernido,

CLXXV
THE DEATH OF ABEL MARTÍN

Thinking he could not see
because God was not watching him,
Abel said as he was dying,
"Whatever it was is over."

—J. de Mairena, *Epigrams*

I

The last swifts are whirling
around the belfry;
children are shouting, jumping, fighting.
Martín, the solitary, alone in his corner.
Evening, nearly nightfall, dust-laden,
the uproar of children, twelve-year-old
voices in his fifty-year-old ears.

*

Oh, full soul and empty spirit,
facing the smoky bonfire
with crackling root-fed flames,
a frontier beacon,
lighting up deep scars!

*

"Live yourself and lose yourself", said Abel.
Oh, distance, distance, guided by
the untouched star!
Who can steer without it?
Distance for the eye —oh, distant ship!—
absence to the hardened heart,

y bálsamo suave
con la miel del amor, sagrado olvido.
¡Oh gran saber del cero, del maduro
fruto sabor que sólo el hombre gusta,
agua de sueño, manantial oscuro,
sombra divina de la mano augusta!
Antes me llegue, si me llega, el Día,
la luz que ve, increada,
ahógame esta mala gritería,
Señor, con las esencias de tu Nada.

V

Y sucedió a la angustia la fatiga,
que siente su esperar desesperado,
la sed que el agua clara no mitiga,
la amargura del tiempo envenenado.
¡Esta lira de muerte!
      Abel palpaba
su cuerpo enflaquecido.
¿El que todo lo ve no le miraba?
¡Y esta pereza, sangre del olvido!
¡Oh, sálvame Señor!
      Su vida entera,
su historia irremediable aparecía
escrita en blanda cera.
¿Y ha de borrarte el sol del nuevo día?
Abel tendió su mano
hacia la luz bermeja
de una caliente aurora de verano,
ya en el balcón de su morada vieja.
Ciego, pidió la luz que no veía.
Luego llevó, sereno,
el limpio vaso, hasta su boca fría,
de pura sombra —¡oh pura sombra!— lleno.

and gentle balm
with the honey of love, blessed oblivion.
Oh, deep wisdom of the zero, savour
of mature fruit for man alone to taste,
dream-water, dark spring,
divine shadow of the mighty hand!
Rather let my Day come—if it does—
with its uncreated, seeing light,
drown out my wicked outcry, Lord,
with the essences of your Nothing.

V

And after anguish came fatigue,
feeling his despairing waiting,
the thirst fresh water cannot quench,
the bitterness of poisoned time.
This lyre of death!
                              Abel felt
his shrivelled body.
Was the All-seeing not watching him?
And this lethargy, oblivion's blood!
Oh, save me, Lord!
                              He saw
his entire life, now done, his story
carved into soft wax—
must the new day's sun melt you away?
Abel held out his hand
toward the vermilion light
of a hot summer dawn,
now reached the balcony of his old house.
Blind, he asked for the light he could not see.
Then calmly raised
to his cold lips the clear glass
filled with purest shadow—oh, pure shadow!

LXXVI S
LA MUERTE DEL NIÑO HERIDO

Otra vez es la noche . . . Es el martillo
de la fiebre en las sienes bien vendadas
del niño. —Madre, ¡el pájaro amarillo!
¡Las mariposas negras y moradas!
       —Duerme, hijo mío. Y la manita oprime
la madre, junto al lecho. —¡Oh flor de fuego!
¿Quién ha de helarte, flor de sangre, dime?
Hay en la pobre alcoba olor de espliego;
       fuera la oronda luna que blanquea
cúpula y torre a la ciudad sombría.
Invisible avión moscardonea.
       —¿Duermes, oh dulce flor de sangre mía?
El cristal del balcón repiquetea.
—¡Oh, fría, fría, fría, fría, fría!

LXXVI S
THE DEATH OF THE WOUNDED CHILD

Once more it's night-time. . . . Fever
hammers in the boy's well-bandaged
temples. "Mother, the yellow bird!
Black and purple butterflies!"
    "Sleep," my child. The mother by the bedside
squeezes his little hand. "Oh, burning flower!
Who will heal you, blood-flower, tell me?"
The bare alcove is scented with lavender;
    outside, the full round moon blanches
the domes and towers of the gloomy city.
An invisible aeroplane buzzes.
    "Are you asleep, sweet flower of my blood?"
The balcony windowpanes rattle.
    Oh, cold, cold, cold, cold, cold!

LXXXIV S
EL CRIMEN FUE EN GRANADA:
A FEDERICO GARCÍA LORCA

1. El crimen
Se le vio, caminando entre fusiles,
por una calle larga,
salir al campo frío,
aún con estrellas de la madrugada.
Mataron a Federico
cuando la luz asomaba.
El pelotón de verdugos
no osó mirarle la cara.
Todos cerraron los ojos;
rezaron: ¡ni Dios te salva!
Muerto cayó Federico
—sangre en la frente y plomo en las entrañas—
. . . Que fue en Granada el crimen
sabed —¡pobre Granada!—, en su Granada.

2. El poeta y la muerte
Se le vio caminar solo con Ella,
sin miedo a su guadaña.
—Ya el sol en torre y torre, los martillos
en yunque— yunque y yunque de las fraguas.
Hablaba Federico,
requebrando a la muerte. Ella escuchaba.
"Porque ayer en mi verso, compañera,
sonaba el golpe de tus secas palmas,
y diste el hielo a mi cantar, y el filo
a mi tragedia de tu hoz de plata,
te cantaré la carne que no tienes,
los ojos que te faltan,
tus cabellos que el viento sacudía,
los rojos labios donde te besaban . . .

LXXXIV S
THE CRIME TOOK PLACE IN GRANADA:
TO FEDERICO GARCÍA LORCA[22]

1. The Crime
He was seen, walking between rifles
down a long street,
out into the cold country
where dawn stars still shone.
They killed Federico
as daylight broke.
The firing-squad soldiers
dared not look him in the face.
They all closed their eyes;
prayed, "Even God can't save you!"
Federico fell dead—
blood on his brow and lead in his guts. . . .
And the crime took place in Granada:
take note—poor Granada, his Granada!

2. The poet and death
He was seen walking alone with Her,
unafraid of her scythe—
with the sun now shining on tower after tower, hammers
on anvils, anvil upon anvil in the forges.
Federico spoke,
flirting with Death. She listened.
"Since, comrade, yesterday you gave my verse
the clap of your dry palms
and put ice in my song, the sharp blade
of your silver sickle in my plays;
so I shall sing you your missing flesh,
your eyeless sockets,
your hair tossed by the wind,
the red lips people kissed. . . .

Hoy como ayer, gitana, muerte mía,
qué bien contigo a solas,
por estos aires de Granada, ¡mi Granada!"

3.
Se le vio caminar . . .

                         Labrad, amigos,
de piedra y sueño en el Alhambra,
un túmulo al poeta,
sobre una fuente donde llore el agua,
y eternamente diga:
el crimen fue en Granada, ¡en su Granada!

Today, as yesterday, gypsy girl, my death,
it's so good alone with you
in these breezes of Granada, my Granada!"

3.
He was seen walking. . . .
                    Friends, carve
a tomb of stone and dreams
for the poet, in the Alhambra,
by a fountain where weeping water
can evermore say:
"The crime took place in Granada, his Granada!"

Notes to the Poems

1   I *THE TRAVELLER.*
Emigration to Latin America for economic reasons was a common feature of late-nineteenth-century Spain. Many, like the brother in this poem, returned disappointed. The image of his youth as **she-wolf** is presumably a reference to the she-wolf that suckled Romulus and Remus and so helped found Rome. The younger brother's "she-wolf" has died without producing successors.

2   VIII *I listen to the songs.*
In his collection of notes on his poems, published in 1924 in *Los complementarios*, Machado wrote of this poem, written in 1898, that "it proclaims the right of lyric poetry to tell of pure feeling, erasing the whole of human history. The volume *Soledades* was the first Spanish book from which the anecdotal had been completely proscribed." Manuel Alvar (ed.), *Los complementarios* (Madrid, 1980), p. 137, cited in his introduction to the latest edition of *Poesías completas* (Madrid, 2000), p. 13.

3   IX BANKS OF THE DUERO
Poplars—*chopos* and *álamos*: Botanically, the two species of poplar most planted around Soria at the present time are *Populus x canadensis* "Robusta," widely seen by roads and planted in lines and clumps as windbreaks, and *Populus* "Italica," the Lombardy Poplar, which lines the Duero banks. The former especially has beautiful bronze leaves in spring, but it is a more recent introduction. Contemporary photographs of the Duero banks show Lombardy Poplars. It is more likely that Machado interchanged the two names for rhythm and assonance than that he made a botanical distinction. In English, "black poplar," "white poplar," and "grey poplar" give variation with rhythm, but unfortunately none of them would accurately translate either *chopo* or *álamo* or be found around Soria.

4   XLVI The waterwheel
The type of **waterwheel** referred to is one where a mule walks round in circles attached to a shaft, which is geared to a series of buckets in which the water is raised from a well. It is Arabic in origin and can still be found in parts of Andalusia.

5   LVIII GLOSS
Manrique: Jorge Manrique (1440–79) is known for the *Coplas que fizo por la muerte de su padre* (Verses he made on the death of his father), from

which the quotation is taken. They express the *planctus* or lament for the passing of all things and the general levelling brought about by death. He took up arms in support of the Infanta Isabel and was killed in action fighting against the troops of one of the nobles who refused to support her and Ferdinand. His father, Rodrigo Manrique, Count of Paredes, was a distinguished soldier, often referred to as "the Second Cid."

6   XCVII PORTRAIT.
The poem dates from 1906, and so acts as a Prelude to the new collection.
Don Juan is the more familiar embodiment of the heartless seducer. Machado cites the original, Don Juan de Mañara, protagonist of Tirso de Molina's *El Burlador de Sevilla*. The Marquess of Bradomín is a later embodiment, whose "memoirs" form the four *Sonatas* (1902–5; one for each season and for each age of life) by Ramón María del Valle-Inclán (1869–1935). Bradomín describes himself as "an ugly, Catholic, and sentimental Don Juan," so Machado might be said to be disclaiming all these attributes.
Rebel blood: the original refers to the radicals of the French revolution in 1789; again, a more generic term seemed preferable.
Ronsard: Pierre de Ronsard (1524–85), the French poet who more than any other represented the Renaissance in French literature, so a "modern" in the sense of post-medieval sensibility. He is contrasted here with the "Modernists" of the early twentieth century —though Machado admired Rubén Darío (1867–1916), as well as having cause to be grateful to him for paying for his and Leonor's return to Soria when she showed the first symptoms of her illness in Brittany in 1911.

7   XCVIII ON THE BANKS OF THE DUERO
Rodrigo of Vivar, "El Cid Campeador," hero of the epic *Poema* (or *Cantar*) *de mío Cid*, written in the mid-twelfth century, some forty years after the death of El Cid in 1099. He was a knight of the minor nobility who fought both against the Moors and at one time for the Moorish king of Zaragoza. He conquered Valencia for King Alfonso VI in 1094. His feats of arms are tempered with moderation and magnanimity to an unusual degree for an epic hero.

8   CXIII AROUND SORIA
I   **Moncayo:** the highest peak (about 7,000 feet) on the eastern horizon from Soria, some thirty-five miles distant, south of the main road to Zaragoza, clearly visible from the hill on which the ruined castle stands. The area surrounding it is now a national park.

VI **Pure Soria:** The implication of *Soria pura* is that the town had no convert inhabitants in the Middle Ages, that they were all "old Christians" (see section IX of this poem) and so of "pure blood." The expression *cristianos viejos* derives from the late Middle Ages, when those who could trace their Christian ancestry back four generations considered themselves superior to and enjoyed privileges denied to the "new Christian" converts from Islam or Judaism and their descendants.

9   VI **Head of Extremadura**: "Extremadura" was in the Middle Ages a general term for reconquered territory bordering that still held by the Moors, so wider than the present province in south-western Spain. More specifically, it marked the extent of *trashumancia*, the movement of flocks of sheep to take advantage of the seasons. Sheep were moved from the present region of Extremadura into northern Castile in the spring. They were shorn there, producing a prosperous wool trade, and pastured during the summer, being moved back south for the autumn and winter. Soria was the farthest point of this migration, and so "head" of Extremadura. The whole phrase, *Soria pura, cabeza de Extremadura*, features on the coat of arms of Soria. (**Cold Soria** needs only a visit outside the summer months to understand.)
    The court house clock: *La Audiencia* stands at the far end of the Plaza Mayor (see Fig 14, p.44). Formerly the courthouse and at one time also the prison, it is now a cultural centre. A fine late Renaissance building, it was built as the Town Hall, but was later replaced as such by the larger seventeenth-century "Los Doce Linajes" building, which stands on the right-hand side of the *plaza* (as you face the *Audiencia*). The bell hangs from a wrought iron structure above the round clock. The church in which Antonio and Leonor were married, Nuestra Señora la Mayor, is also in this square.

10 VIII **San Polo and San Saturio**: These two shrines (see Figs 12 and 15, pp. 42, 44) stand on the eastern bank of the river Duero, connected by the poplar-lined track that was one of Machado's favourite walks and major inspirations. San Polo, opposite the old city walls and the site of the castle, was originally a Templar monastery and was the inspiration for Gustavo Adolfo Bécquer's poem *El rayo de luna*. St Polus, who may or may not have been a historical figure, is now only commemorated locally. St Saturius was a hermit "of Numantia," according to the latest Roman Martyrology, who died in 606. He is the patron saint of Soria. The present building, clinging to the rock face about half a mile south of San Polo, dates from the eighteenth century but is supposedly over the site of Saturius' hermit's cave. The interior is covered in frescoes by the eighteenth-century Sorian painter Antonio Zapata. The annual festival of *Las Bailas* is held on the terrace across the river from San Saturio (where the translators had the pleasure of shaking the wet paw of a large black dog named Laika, who swims across the river every day of the year).

11 IX **High Numantian plain**: Four miles north-east of Soria is the site of Numantia, where a Celtiberian fortress was defended against the occupying Roman army for twenty years, at the end of which, in 133 BCE, the remaining inhabitants all took their own lives rather than surrender to the Roman commander Scipio Africanus the Younger. This heroic resistance has something of the same symbolic importance for Spain that

Masada has for the Jews. *Numantia* is the Latin name given to the site after the conquest, and the ruins that can be seen there are mainly those of the Roman town built on the site rather than of the Celtiberian settlement.

12   CXV TO A WITHERED ELM
The old elm, now filled with concrete and quite dead (see Fig. 17, p.88), stands just inside the churchyard of Santa María del Espino, beside the cemetery. In the final stages of Leonor's illness, when she could no longer walk, Antonio would lift her into a handcart and push her round the streets to give her some fresh air, often passing this tree. The "other miracle from spring" would be her recovery, which he must have known to be impossible.

13   CXVII TO THE MASTER AZORÍN
Azorín: The pen name of José Martínez Ruiz (1873–1967), essayist and one of the most influential thinkers of the Generation of '98. With the 1912 letter Machado wrote to Juan Ramón Jiménez following the publication of *Campos de Castilla*, he enclosed a copy of this poem, with the comment: "I am sending you this composition to the book *Castilla* by Azorín so that you can see the direction I am considering giving this section [included in later editions of *Campos de Castilla*]. In it I am trying to place myself at the point of departure of a few select souls and to continue in myself these various impulses on a common course, towards an ideal and distant look This book of Azorín's, so intense, so laden with soul, has stirred my spirit deeply and its influence is not —far from it— exhausted in this piece."
Cidones Inn: The inn is still there, eight miles west of Soria, externally little changed (see Fig. 19, p.91). It had a period (1970s and 1980s) of paying homage to Machado for the tourist trade he brought it, with a copy of the poem on the wall and various photographs of the period. The latest interior refurbishment, however, seems to have left him forgotten. It still (2001) provides an excellent local menu at very reasonable prices.
The gentleman is young and dressed in mourning: Machado himself. Waiting for the mail coach at the inn has been described as a displaced re-creation of his own departure from Soria after Leonor's death, on the horse-drawn carriage, known as "la pajarilla," that took him to the railway station. See J. Montero Padilla, *Antonio Machado en su Geografía* (Segovia, 1995), p. 48.

14   CXXVI TO JOSÉ MARÍA PALACIO
José María Palacio was a journalist in Soria who became a close friend of Machado. He owned and edited the newspaper *El porvenir castellano*, in which this poem was first published in 1916.
The Espino: The cemetery in which Leonor is buried is attached to the church of Santa María del Espino (see note 12 to Poem CXV *To a Withered Elm* above).

15   CXXIX NOVEMBER 1913.
From Baeza, where this poem was written, the **Sierra de Cazorla** is
some thirty miles east and the **Mágina** and **Aznaitín** ranges are to the
south, all rising to well over 6,000 feet. **Granada** lies about fifty miles
farther south.

16   CXXX THE *SAETA*
The *saeta* is a popular form of *flamenco* song (the Spanish word literally
meaning "arrow"), "shot" from balconies in praise of the figures of Jesus,
the Virgin, and other saints carried in Holy Week processions in
Andalusia.

17   CXXXI THE EPHEMERAL PAST
The **provincial casino** may well have been inspired by the Casino de
Numancia, which still flourishes in Soria's main *paseo*, the Calle El
Collado (see Fig. 18, p.90). It was the centre of social life in Soria at the
time Machado was there and had been the scene for the first
performance of an "impromptu gallop" for piano, written to celebrate the
opening of the Torralba-Soria railway link.
Carancha: José Sánchez del Campo, known as *Cara-Ancha* (broad-face)
was a famous bullfighter of the late nineteenth century. Born in 1848, he
retired in 1894. His great rivals of the time were Lagartijo and Frascuelo
(see note to Poem CXXXV *The Ephemeral Future*, below). In
competition with them, he revived the difficult move of killing the bull
"**receiving**," i.e. allowing the bull to charge the sword so that its own
impetus sinks the sword (as opposed to the more usual "thrust" over the
stationary bull's horns). The first time he did this was on 19 June 1881,
and the occasion became so famous that it was commented on and
discussed all over Spain for many years. So the **once** in this line can be
assigned a particular date, pre-1898, in the full era of **brass bands and
tambourines** that Machado is here castigating. (Information from M.P.
Palomo, *Antonio Machado. Poesía*, Madrid: Narcea, 1971, p. 227, relying on
J.M. de Cossío, *Los Toros*, vol. II, Madrid, 1943, p. 884).
Cordobés: stiff, low-crowned hat, traditional to Andalusia, worn on
horseback, recalling bullfights and *ferias*.

18   CXXXV THE EPHEMERAL FUTURE
Frascuelo: Salvador Sánchez Frascuelo was born in Granada in 1842 and
died in 1898. He was particularly associated with the Chinchón district
of Madrid, especially after he was badly gored in the ring there in 1863
and nursed for three months in a house known as Tío Tamayo's. In
gratitude, he inaugurated a festival for old and sick inhabitants of
Chinchón, the first of its kind in Spain. Known as a *bon viveur* in later
life, he was on intimate terms with King Alfonso XII.

19   CXXXIX FOR DON FRANCISCO GINER DE LOS RÍOS
Francisco Giner de los Ríos: Born in 1839 in Ronda (or possibly
Málaga), he studied law at Granada University before moving to Madrid.

There he came under the influence of Julián Sanz del Río, who introduced the works of the German philosopher Karl Krause to Spain. *Krausismo* emphasized development of the individual and became the inspiration behind Giner's educational theories. In 1876 he founded the *Instituto Libre de Enseñanza*, the Free Teaching Institute (meaning free from church and state influence), which Antonio Machado and most of the influential members of the Generation of '98 attended and remembered with gratitude. He published a number of volumes of essays on art, literature, philosophy and law. He died in Madrid on 17 February 1915, so this poem was written five days after his death.

20   LXXXVII OH, GUADALQUIVIR...
Sanlúcar: Sanlúcar de Barrameda, on the Costa de la Luz (Coast of Light), where the river Guadalquivir flows into the Atlantic, about thirty miles south west of Seville. It rises in the southern part of the Sierra de **Cazorla**, just north of the peak of Cabañas (2,028 metres; about 6,300 feet).

21   CLXV — IV
This sonnet (written in 1924) is largely a reworking of an earlier poem, dated 13 March 1916 but not published till 1956. It bears the epigraph "*In time. 1882. 1890. 1892. My father.*" 1882 was the family's last year in Seville, and the poet's final memories of his father there are evoked in the 1916 poem's images of him in the garden and the library:

> *Mi padre en el jardín de nuestra casa,*
> *mi padre, entre sus libros, trabajando.*
> *Los ojos grandes, la alta frente,*
> *el rostro enjuto, los bigotes lacios.*
> *Mi padre escribe (letra diminuta),*
> *medita, sueña, sufre, habla alto.*
> *Pasea —oh, padre mío, ¡todavía*
> *estás ahí, el tiempo no te ha borrado!*

> My father in the garden of our house,
> my father working among his books.
> Large eyes, lofty brow,
> lean face, drooping moustache.
> My father writes (tiny writing),
> Thinks, dreams, suffers, speaks out loud.
> He walks—oh, my father, you are
> still here; time has not erased you!

By 1890, Antonio was fourteen and well able to appreciate the family's fading fortunes and to see the advance of his father's illness. 1892 was the last year in which he saw his father, who returned from Puerto Rico mortally ill the following year. Antonio's mother went to be with him in Seville, but the five children stayed in Madrid.

It has been suggested that the sonnet reflects the influence of Azorín (for further details see Montero Padilla, *Antonio Machado en su Geografía*, pp. 26–9).

22   LXXXIV S THE CRIME TOOK PLACE IN GRANADA
Federico García Lorca was shot outside Granada on 18 August 1936. He had returned to his home town from Madrid on 14 July, to find a city in a state of turmoil, with acts of violence being committed by opposing bands of Falangists and trade unionists. The army garrison rebelled against the Republican government on 20 July, two days after General Franco's broadcast announcing the "National Crusade" against the "Reds"—made, ironically, on the feast of St Frederick (bishop of Utrecht and martyr; died 838), which the García Lorca family marked by holding an open day for father and eldest son, both named after the saint. The leader of the rebel officers was Juan Valdés Guzmán, to whom the primary responsibility for Lorca's death must be attributed. On 10 August Lorca left the family home and took refuge in central Granada with the family of a poet friend, Luis Rosales, in a house that seemed safe as two of his brothers were leading Falangists. But his whereabouts were discovered, and he was arrested on 16 August. He was taken to the Civil Government building, where efforts by the Rosales family to get him released as being "politically harmless" all failed. For Valdés he was a dangerous "Red", like virtually all writers and other intellectuals —and a known homosexual, to make matters worse. The following day he was taken out of the town to a former children's holiday colony, Villa Concha, known "La Colonia," above the village of Víznar, which had become a last holding place for prisoners on their way to execution. From there, before sunrise the following morning, he was driven along the road to Alfacar. The lorry stopped by the spring known to the Arabs as Ainadamar and to the Spanish as Fuente Grande. There Federico, two minor bullfighters, and a village schoolteacher were shot. The fullest possible account of his last days and death can be found in the final chapter of Ian Gibson, *Federico García Lorca: A Life* (London and Boston: Faber and Faber, 1989), pp. 446–70, from which this summary is taken.

   Machado gives his elegy deliberate echoes of Lorca's own poems dealing with death: the opening lines are reminiscent of "Death of Antoñito Camborio" and "Ballad of the Spanish Civil Guard," while the second part recalls the "Lament for the Death of Ignacio Sánchez Mejías." See *Federico García Lorca: Gypsy Ballads* (Romancero Gitano), trans. Robert G. Havard (Warminster, 1990), pp. 86–9, 98–105.

Selected Bibliography

Aguirre, J. M. *Antonio Machado, poeta simbolista* (Madrid: Taurus, 1973).

Albornoz, Aurora de. *La presencia de Miguel de Unamuno en Antonio Machado* (Madrid: Gredos, 1968).

Alonso, Dámaso. "Poesías olvidadas de Antonio Machado," in *Cuadernos Hispanoamericanos*, Nos. 11-12 (Madrid, 1949).

Aranguren, José Luis. "Esperanza y desesperanza de Dios en la experiencia de Antonio Machado," in *Cuadernos Hispanoamericanos*, Nos. 11-12 (Madrid, 1949).

Bousoño, Carlos. *Teoría de la expresión poética* (Madrid: Gredos, 1956).

Cano, José Luis. "Antonio Machado, hombre y poeta en sueños," in *Cuadernos Hispanoamericanos*, Nos. 11-12 (Madrid, 1949).

------. *Antonio Machado. Antología poética. Bibliografía* (Barcelona: Bruguera, 1982).

Cernuda, Luis. *Estudios sobre poesía española contemporánea* (Madrid: Guadarrama, 1958).

Cobos, Pablo A. "Antonio Machado en Segovia. Vida y obra," (Madrid: Insula, 1973)

Darío, Rubén. "Los hermanos Machado," in *La Nación* (Buenos Aires), 15 June 1909.

Díaz-Plaja, Guillermo. *Modernismo frente a Noventa y Ocho* (Madrid: Espasa-Calpe, 1951).

Diego, Gerardo. "Tempo lento en Antonio Machado," in *Cuadernos Hispanoamericanos*, Nos. 11-12 (Madrid, 1949).

Espina, Concha. *De Antonio Machado a su grande y secreto amor* (Madrid: Gráficas Reunidas, 1950).

Gullón, Ricardo. *Las secretas galerías de Antonio Machado* (Madrid: Taurus, 1958).

------. *Relaciones entre Antonio Machado y Juan Ramón Jiménez* (Pisa, University of Pisa, 1964).

------. and Allen W. Phillips, *Antonio Machado, el escritor y la crítica* (Madrid: Taurus, 1973).

Jiménez, Juan Ramón. "Antonio Machado," in *Insula* 144 (Madrid), 15 Nov. 1958.

Laín Entralgo, Pedro. *La Generación del Noventa y Ocho* (Buenos Aires: Espasa-Calpe, 1947).

Machado, José. *Ultimas soledades del poeta Antonio Machado* (Soria: Imprenta Provincial, 1971).

Marías, Julián. "La poesía de Antonio Machado y su interpretación poética de las cosas," in *Cuadernos Hispanoamericanos*, Nos. 11-12 (Madrid, 1949).

McVan, Alice Jane. *Antonio Machado* (New York: The Hispanic Society of America, 1959).

Moreno Villa, José. *Las cinco palabras de Antonio Machado* (México, Leyendo a, El colegio de México, 1944).

Peers, E. Allison. *Antonio Machado* (Oxford: Clarendon Press, 1940).

Pérez Ferrero, Miguel. *Vida de Antonio Machado y Manuel* (Madrid: Espasa-Calpe, 1952).

Ribbans, Geoffrey. "Antonio Machado's *Soledades*: A Critical Study," in *Hispanic Review*, XXX, (July 1962).

------. *La poesía de Antonio Machado antes de llegar a Soria* (Soria: Publicaciones de la Cátedra de Antonio Machado, 1962).

------. "La influencia de Verlaine en Antonio Machado," in *Cuadernos Hispanoamericanos*, Nos. 91-92 (Madrid, Jul-Aug 1957).

Rodriguez Aguilar, Cesáreo. *Antonio Machado en Baeza* (Barcelona: Ediciones A. P., 1968).

Ruiz de Conde, Justina. "Antonio Machado y Guiomar," (Madrid, Insula, 1964

Sánchez Barbudo, Antonio. *Estudios sobre Unamuno y Machado* (Madrid: Guadarrama, 1959).

------. *Los poemas de Antonio Machado* (Barcelona: Lumen, 1967).

Serrano Poncela, Segundo. *Antonio Machado: su mundo y su obra* (Buenos Aires: Losada, 1954).

Torre, Guillermo de. "Antonio Machado y sus poetas apócrifos," in *Insula* 126 (Madrid), 15 May 1957).

Trend, J. B. *Antonio Machado* (Oxford: Dolphin Book Co., 1953).

Tuñón de Lara, Manuel. *Antonio Machado, poeta del pueblo* (Madrid: Gredos, 1955).

Zubiría, Ramón de. *La poesía de Antonio Machado* (Madrid: Gredos, 1955).

Translations

Prose

Juan de Mairena: Epigrams, Maxims, Memoranda, and Memoirs of an Apocryphal Professor. With an Appendix of Poems from the Apocryphal Songbooks. Tr. by Ben Belitt (Berkeley and Los Angeles: University of California Press, 1963).

Poetry: Collections

Antonio Machado: Selected Poems. Tr. by Alan S. Trueblood (Cambridge, Mass. and London: Harvard University Press, 1982).

Castilian Ilexes. Tr. by Charles Tomlinson and Henry Gifford (New York and London: Oxford University Press, 1963).

The Dream Below the Sun. Tr. by Willis Barnstone. Trumansberg (New York: The Crossing Press, 1981).

Eighty Poems. Tr. by Willis Barnstone (New York: Las Américas, 1959).

I Go Dreaming Roads. Tr. by Carmen Scholes and William Witherup. (Monterey, CA: Peters Gate Press, 1973).

"Poems." Tr. by Colin Falck. In Colin Falck, *The Garden of the Evening* (Oxford: The Review [Pamphlet Series, no. 1], 1964).

Poems of Exchange: With Six Poems Translated from the Spanish of Antonio Machado. Tr. by Willis Barnstone (Athens, 1951).

Sea of San Juan. Tr. by Eleonor L. Turnbull (Boston: Humphries, 1950).

"Selected Poems." Tr. by Alice Jane McVan. In Alice Jane McVan, *Antonio Machado* (New York: Hispanic Society of America, 1959).
Selected Poems of Antonio Machado. Tr. by Betty Jean Craige (Baton Rouge and London: Louisiana State University Press,1978).
Sunlight and Scarlet: Selected Poems. Tr. by Ivor Waters (Chepstow: I. Waters, 1973).
Times Alone. Selected Poems of Antonio Machado. Tr. by Robert Bly (Middletown, Connecticut: Wesleyan University Press, 1983).
Thirty Spanish Poems of Love and Exile. Tr. by Kenneth Rexroth. (San Francisco: City Lights, 1955).
Zero. Tr. by Eleonor L. Turnbull (Baltimore: Contemporary Poetry, Distinguished Poets Series, 1947).

Printed and bound by CPI Group (UK) Ltd, Croydon, CR0 4YY

13/04/2025

14656604-0005